Visions of Fantasy

Visions
of Fantasy
Tales from the Masters

Edited by

Isaac Asimov and Martin H. Greenberg

Illustrated by Larry Elmore

DOUBLEDAY

NEW YORK   LONDON   TORONTO   SYDNEY   AUCKLAND

ACKNOWLEDGMENTS

"The Smallest Dragonboy" by Anne McCaffrey. Copyright © 1974 by Anne McCaffrey; reprinted by permission of the author and the author's agent, Virginia Kidd.

"A Message from Charity" by William Lee. Copyright © 1967 by Mercury Press, Inc. From *The Magazine of Fantasy and Science Fiction.* Reprinted by permission of the Scott Meredith Literary Agency, Inc., 845 Third Avenue, New York, NY 10022.

"The Seventh Mandarin" by Jane Yolen. Copyright © 1970 by Jane Yolen. Reprinted by permission of Curtis Brown, Ltd.

"The Voices of El Dorado" by Howard Goldsmith. Copyright © 1974 by Howard Goldsmith. Reprinted by permission of the author.

"The Box" by Bruce Coville. Copyright © 1986 by Bruce Coville. Reprinted by permission of the author.

"The Lake" by Ray Bradbury. Copyright © 1944, renewed 1972 by Ray Bradbury. Reprinted by permission of Don Congdon Associates, Inc.

"A Dozen of Everything" by Marion Zimmer Bradley. Copyright © 1959 by Ziff-Davis Publications, Inc.; renewed © 1987 by Marion Zimmer Bradley. Reprinted by permission of the Scott Meredith Literary Agency, Inc., 845 Third Avenue, New York, NY 10022.

"Poor Little Saturday" by Madeleine L'Engle. Copyright © 1956 by King-Size Publications; renewed © 1984 by Madeleine L'Engle. Reprinted by permission of Lescher & Lescher, Ltd.

"The Fable of the Three Princes" by Isaac Asimov. Copyright © 1987 by Nightfall, Inc. Reprinted by permission of the author.

"Letters from Camp" by Al Sarrantonio. Copyright © 1981 by Al Sarrantonio. Reprinted by permission of the author.

"Things That Go Quack in the Night" by Lewis and Edith Shiner. Copyright © 1983 by Davis Publications, Inc. First published in *Isaac Asimov's Science Fiction Magazine.* Reprinted by permission of the authors.

"Voices in the Wind" by Elizabeth S. Helfman. Copyright © 1987 by Elizabeth S. Helfman. Reprinted by permission of the author.

Published by Doubleday, a division of Bantam Doubleday Dell Publishing Group, Inc., 666 Fifth Avenue, New York, New York 10103

Doubleday and the portrayal of an anchor with a dolphin are trademarks of Doubleday, a division of Bantam Doubleday Dell Publishing Group, Inc.

Library of Congress Cataloging-in-Publication Data

Visions of fantasy: tales from the masters / edited by Isaac Asimov and Martin H. Greenberg: illustrated by Larry Elmore.—1st ed.
 p.   cm.
 Contents: The smallest dragonboy / by Anne McCaffrey—A message from charity / by William Lee—The seventh mandarin—by Jane Yolen—The voices of El Dorado / by Howard Goldsmith—The box / by Bruce Coville—The lake / by Ray Bradbury—A dozen of everything / by Marion Zimmer Bradley—Poor little Saturday / by Madeleine L'Engle—The fable of the three princes / by Isaac Asimov—Letters from camp / by Al Sarrantonio —Things that go quack in the night / by Lewis and Edith Shiner—Voices in the wind / by Elizabeth S. Helfman.
 1. Children's stories, American. [1. Fantasy. 2. Short stories.] I. Asimov, Isaac, 1920– . II. Greenberg, Martin Harry. III. Elmore, Larry, ill.
PZ5.V474 1989
[Fic]—dc20 89-7917 CIP AC
ISBN: 0-385-26359-7

Copyright © 1989 by Isaac Asimov and Martin H. Greenberg
Illustrations © 1989 by Doubleday, a division of
Bantam Doubleday Dell Publishing Group, Inc.
All Rights Reserved

Printed in the United States of America
October 1989
First Edition

Contents

Introduction

In its broadest sense, a fantasy is any work of the imagination, any story that never really happened, but is made up by the storyteller.

For instance, if you say, "My brother John went to the store," and John had indeed gone to the store, that is a *fact.*

If you say, "My brother John went to the store," and actually he didn't, but you honestly *thought* he did, that is a *mistake.*

If you say, "My brother John went to the store," and actually he didn't, and you *know* that he didn't, that is a *lie.*

Suppose, though, that you're making up an exciting story. You know it really didn't happen, and the person you're telling it to knows it really didn't happen. You begin, "My brother John went to the store—" Now you're telling a story, something that's *fiction.*

Any story at all is a fantasy because it's coming out of your imagination, but the term is used especially for a certain kind of fiction.

Suppose the story starts as follows: "My brother John went to the store and on the way he met an old man wearing a gray hat." That would just be a *story*. It didn't happen, but it *might* have happened. After all, old men wearing gray hats do exist and why shouldn't your brother have met one of them?

But suppose the story starts as follows: "My brother John went to the store and on the way he met a dragon with orange wings." Now, not only did that not happen, but it *couldn't* happen, because there are no dragons with orange wings that anyone can possibly meet on the way to a store or anywhere else. The story you are now telling is a *fantasy.*

Ordinary fiction is a story that isn't true, but might be. Fantasy is a story that isn't true, and *can't* be.

In ancient times, when people didn't know much about the world, fantasy wasn't really fantasy. It was just fiction. Most people were quite ready to believe that dragons did exist, as well as giants and ogres, or witches and wizards, or ghosts and demons, or unicorns and fairies, and so on.

With time, though, people discovered that all these things —and many others—simply didn't exist, and fantasies grew less popular. People went about saying, "Oh, that's just a fairy story" and would dismiss it. This was a shame because fantasies are very exciting, and when you're shivering over the villainy of a wicked witch, it's annoying to be told, "Witches don't exist, you know."

Nowadays, therefore, fantasies are often written for young people because the world is new to them, and their imaginations are still so active. They are ready to believe in dragons and fairies and all the rest, and they can still enjoy fantasies.

But, if you stop to think of it, grown-ups can enjoy fantasies, too, provided they are willing to forget that some things are really impossible for just the short time that they are reading a story or listening to one. This is called "suspension of disbelief." For just a little while, you can stop disbelieving in unicorns and ghosts, for instance.

This is important because although it is young people who most enjoy fantasies, it is grown-ups who write them. A grown-up who is writing a fantasy has to pretend or suppose that he's writing about things that could really happen. This is so he can make a fantasy about even the wildest things *sound* real. He has to do that to make the story seem truly interesting and exciting.

A fantasy writer can write something that is very old-fashioned, and is all about princes, princesses, and spells, and still make it sound real. I've written a story like that, which is included in this book. It is "The Fable of the Three Princes."

Or a fantasy writer can just hint at something that is mysterious and dangerous, as Al Sarrantonio does in "Letters from Camp."

In fact, we have twelve stories by twelve different writers, and each one is a different kind of fantasy. Each one will show you, whether it is funny or scary, exciting or mysterious, that fantasy is *fun* and that it can be quite modern, too.

—ISAAC ASIMOV
New York, March 1989

The Smallest Dragonboy

Anne McCaffrey

ALTHOUGH KEEVAN lengthened his walking stride as far as his legs would stretch, he couldn't quite keep up with the other candidates. He knew he would be teased again.

Just as he knew many things that his foster mother told him he ought not to know, Keevan knew that Beterli, the most senior of the boys, set that spanking pace just to embarrass him, the smallest dragonboy. Keevan would arrive, tail fork-end of the group, breathless, chest heaving, and maybe get a stern look from the instructing wingsecond.

Dragonriders, even if they were still only hopeful candidates for the glowing eggs which were hardening on the hot sands of the Hatching Ground cavern, were expected to be punctual and prepared. Sloth was not tolerated by the Weyrleader of Benden Weyr. A good record was especially important now. It was very near hatching time, when the baby dragons would crack their mottled shells, and stagger forth to choose their lifetime companions. The very thought of that glorious moment made Keevan's breath catch in his throat. To be chosen—to be a dragonrider! To sit astride the neck of a winged beast with jeweled eyes: to be his companion in good times and fighting extremes; to fly effortlessly over the lands of Pern! Or, thrillingly, *between* to any point anywhere on the world! Flying *between* was done on dragonback or not at all, and it was dangerous.

Keevan glanced upward, past the black mouths of the weyr caves in which grown dragons and their chosen riders lived, toward the Star Stones that crowned the ridge of the old volcano that was Benden Weyr. On the height, the blue watch dragon, his rider mounted on his neck, stretched the great transparent pinions that carried him on the winds of Pern to fight the evil Thread that fell at certain times from the skies. The many-faceted rainbow jewels of his eyes glistened fleetingly in the greeny sun. He folded his great wings to his back, and the watchpair resumed their statuelike pose of alertness.

Then the enticing view was obscured as Keevan passed into the Hatching Ground cavern. The sands underfoot were hot, even through heavy wher-hide boots. How the bootmaker had protested having to sew so small! Keevan was forced to wonder why being small was reprehensible. People were always calling him "babe" and shooing him away as being "too small" or "too young" for this or that. Keevan was constantly working, twice as hard as any other boy his age, to prove himself capable. What if his muscles weren't as big as Beterli's? They were just as hard. And if he couldn't overpower anyone in a wrestling match, he could outdistance everyone in a footrace.

"Maybe if you run fast enough," Beterli had jeered on the occasion when Keevan had been goaded to boast of his swiftness, "you could catch a dragon. That's the only way you'll make a dragonrider!"

"You just wait and see, Beterli, you just wait," Keevan had replied. He would have liked to wipe the contemptuous smile from Beterli's face, but the guy didn't fight fair even when a wingsecond was watching. "No one knows what Impresses a dragon!"

"They've got to be able to *find* you first, babe!"

Yes, being the smallest candidate was not an enviable position. It was therefore imperative that Keevan Impress a dragon in his first hatching. That would wipe the smile off every face in the cavern, and accord him the respect due any dragonrider, even the smallest one.

Besides, no one knew exactly what Impressed the baby dragons as they struggled from their shells toward their lifetime partners.

"I like to believe that dragons see into a man's heart," Keevan's foster mother, Mende, told him. "If they find goodness, honesty, a flexible mind, patience, courage—and you've got that in quantity, dear Keevan—that's what dragons look for. I've seen many a well-grown lad left standing on the sands, Hatching Day, in favor of someone not so strong or tall or handsome. And if my memory serves me"—which it usually did: Mende knew every word of every Harper's tale worth telling, Keevan did not interrupt her to say so—"I don't believe that F'lar, our Weyrleader, was all that tall when bronze Mnementh chose him. And Mnementh was the only bronze dragon of that hatching."

Dreams of Impressing a bronze were beyond Keevan's boldest reflections, although that goal dominated the thoughts of every other hopeful candidate. Green dragons were small and fast and more numerous. There was more prestige to Impressing a blue or brown than a green. Being practical, Keevan seldom dreamed as high as a big fighting brown, like Canth, F'nor's fine fellow, the biggest brown on all Pern. But to fly a bronze? Bronzes were almost as big as the queen, and only they took the air when a queen flew at mating time. A bronze rider could aspire to become Weyrleader! Well, Keevan would console himself, brown riders could aspire to become wingseconds, and that wasn't bad. He'd even settle for a green dragon: they were small, but so was he. No matter! He simply had to Impress a dragon his first time in the Hatching Ground. Then no one in the Weyr would taunt him anymore for being so small.

Shells, Keevan thought now, but the sands are hot!

"Impression time is imminent, candidates," the wingsecond was saying as everyone crowded respectfully close to him. "See the extent of the striations on this promising egg?" The stretch marks *were* larger than yesterday.

Everyone leaned forward and nodded thoughtfully. That particular egg was the one Beterli had marked as his own, and no other candidate dared, on pain of being beaten by Beterli at his first opportunity, to approach it. The egg was marked by a large yellowish splotch in the shape of a dragon back-winging to land, talons outstretched to grasp the rock. Everyone knew that bronze eggs bore distinctive markings. And naturally, Beterli, who'd been presented at eight Impressions already and was the biggest of the candidates, had chosen it.

"I'd say that the great opening day is almost upon us," the wingsecond went on, and then his face assumed a grave expression. "As we well know, there are only forty eggs and seventy-two candidates. Some of you may be disappointed on the great day. That doesn't necessarily mean you aren't dragonrider material, just that *the* dragon for you hasn't been shelled. You'll have other hatchings, and it's no disgrace to be left behind an Impression or two. Or more."

Keevan was positive that the wingsecond's eyes rested on Beterli, who'd been stood off at so many Impressions already. Keevan tried to squinch down so the wingsecond wouldn't notice him. Keevan had been reminded too often that he was eligible to be a candidate by one day only. He, of all the hopefuls, was most likely to be left standing on the

4 •

great day. One more reason why he simply had to Impress at his first hatching.

"Now move about among the eggs," the wingsecond said. "Touch them. We don't know that it does any good, but it certainly doesn't do any harm."

Some of the boys laughed nervously, but everyone immediately began to circulate among the eggs. Beterli stepped up officiously to "his" egg, daring anyone to come near it. Keevan smiled, because he had already touched it—every inspection day, when the others were leaving the Hatching Ground and no one could see him crouch to stroke it.

Keevan had an egg he concentrated on, too, one drawn slightly to the far side of the others. The shell had a soft greenish-blue tinge with a faint creamy swirl design. The consensus was that this egg contained a mere green, so Keevan was rarely bothered by rivals. He was somewhat perturbed then to see Beterli wandering over to him.

"I don't know why you're allowed in this Impression, Keevan. There are enough of us without a babe," Beterli said, shaking his head.

"I'm of age." Keevan kept his voice level, telling himself not to be bothered by mere words.

"Yah!" Beterli made a show of standing on his toetips. "You can't even see over an egg; Hatching Day, you better get in front or the dragons won't see you at all. Course, you could get run down that way in the mad scramble. Oh, I forget, you can run fast, can't you?"

"You'd better make sure a dragon sees *you,* this time, Beterli," Keevan replied. "You're almost overage, aren't you?"

Beterli flushed and took a step forward, hand half-raised. Keevan stood his ground, but if Beterli advanced one more step, he would call the wingsecond. No one fought on the Hatching Ground. Surely Beterli knew that much.

Fortunately, at that moment, the wingsecond called the boys together and led them from the Hatching Ground to start on evening chores. There were "glows" to be replenished in the main kitchen caverns and sleeping cubicles, the major hallways, and the queen's apartment. Firestone sacks had to be filled against Thread attack, and black rock brought to the kitchen hearths. The boys fell to their chores, tantalized by the odors of roasting meat. The population of the Weyr began to assemble for the evening meal, and the dragonriders came in from the Feeding Ground on their sweep checks.

It was the time of day Keevan liked best: once the chores were done but before dinner was served, a fellow could often get close enough to the dragonriders to hear their talk. Tonight, Keevan's father, K'last, was at the main dragonriders' table. It puzzled Keevan how his father, a brown rider and a tall man, could *be* his father—because he, Keevan, was so small. It obviously puzzled K'last, too, when he deigned to notice his small son: "In a few more Turns, you'll be as tall as I am—or taller!"

K'last was pouring Benden wine all around the table. The dragonriders were relaxing. There'd be no Thread attack for three more days, and they'd be in the mood to tell tales, better than Harper yarns, about impossible maneuvers they'd done a-dragonback. When Thread attack was closer, their talk would change to a discussion of tactics or evasion, of going *between,* how long to suspend there until the burning but fragile Thread would freeze and crack and fall harmlessly off dragon and man. They would dispute the exact moment to feed firestone to the dragon so he'd have the best flame ready to sear Thread midair and render it harmless to ground—and man—below. There was such a lot to know and understand about being a dragonrider that sometimes Keevan was overwhelmed. How would he ever be able

6 •

to remember everything he ought to know at the right moment? He couldn't dare ask such a question: this would only have given additional weight to the notion that he was too young yet to be a dragonrider.

"Having older candidates makes good sense," L'vel was saying, as Keevan settled down near the table. "Why waste four to five years of a dragon's fighting prime until his rider grows up enough to stand the rigors?" L'vel had Impressed a blue of Ramoth's first clutch. Most of the candidates thought L'vel was marvelous because he spoke up in front of the older riders, who awed them. "That was well enough in the Interval when you didn't need to mount the full Weyr complement to fight Thread. But not now. Not with more eligible candidates than ever. Let the babes wait."

"Any boy who is over twelve Turns has the right to stand in the Hatching Ground," K'last replied, a slight smile on his face. He never argued or got angry. Keevan wished he were more like his father. And oh, how he wished he were a brown rider! "Only a dragon—each particular dragon—knows what he wants in a rider. We certainly can't tell. Time and again the theorists," K'last's smile deepened as his eyes swept those at the table, "are surprised by dragon choice. *They* never seem to make mistakes, however."

"Now, K'last, just look at the roster this Impression. Seventy-two boys and only forty eggs. Drop off the twelve youngest, and there's still a good field for the hatchlings to choose from. Shells! There are a couple of weyrlings unable to see over a wher egg much less a dragon! And years before they can ride Thread."

"True enough, but the Weyr is scarcely under fighting strength, and if the youngest Impress, they'll be old enough to fight when the oldest of our current dragons go *between* from senility."

"Half the Weyr-bred lads have already been through several Impressions," one of the bronze riders said then. "I'd say drop some of *them* off this time."

"There's nothing wrong in presenting a clutch with as wide a choice as possible," said the Weyrleader, who had joined the table with Lessa, the Weyrwoman.

"Has there ever been a case," she said, smiling in her odd way at the riders, "where a hatchling didn't choose?"

Her suggestion was almost heretical and drew astonished gasps from everyone, including the boys.

F'lar laughed. "You say the most outrageous things, Lessa."

"Well, *has* there ever been a case where a dragon didn't choose?"

"Can't say as I recall one," K'last replied.

"Then we continue in this tradition," Lessa said firmly, as if that ended the matter.

But it didn't. The argument ranged from one table to the other all through dinner, with some favoring a weeding out of the candidates to the most likely, lopping off those who were very young or who had had multiple opportunities to Impress. All the candidates were in a swivet, though such a departure from tradition would be to the advantage of many. As the evening progressed, more riders were favoring eliminating the youngest and those who'd passed four or more Impressions unchosen. Keevan felt he could bear such a dictum only if Beterli were also eliminated. But this seemed less likely than that Keevan would be turfed out, since the Weyr's need was for fighting dragons and riders.

By the time the evening meal was over, no decision had been reached, although the Weyrleader had promised to give the matter due consideration.

He might have slept on the problem, but few of the candidates did. Tempers were uncertain in the sleeping caverns next morning as the boys were routed out of their beds to carry water and black rock and cover the "glows." Twice Mende had to call Keevan to order for clumsiness.

"Whatever is the matter with you, boy?" she demanded in exasperation when he tippled black rock short of the bin and sooted up the hearth.

"They're going to keep me from this Impression."

"What?" Mende stared at him. "Who?"

"You heard them talking at dinner last night. They're going to turf the babes from the hatching."

Mende regarded him a moment longer before touching his arm gently. "There's lots of talk around a supper table, Keevan. And it cools as soon as the supper. I've heard the same nonsense before every hatching, but nothing is ever changed."

"There's always a first time," Keevan answered, copying one of her own phrases.

"That'll be enough of that, Keevan. Finish your job. If the clutch does hatch today, we'll need full rock bins for the feast, and you won't be around to do the filling. All my fosterlings make dragonriders."

"The first time?" Keevan was bold enough to ask as he scooted off with the rockbarrow.

Perhaps, Keevan thought later, if he hadn't been on that chore just when Beterli was also fetching black rock, things might have turned out differently. But he had dutifully trundled the barrow to the outdoor bunker for another load just as Beterli arrived on a similar errand.

"Heard the news, babe?" Beterli asked. He was grinning from ear to ear, and he put an unnecessary emphasis on the final insulting word.

"The eggs are cracking?" Keevan all but dropped the loaded shovel. Several anxieties flicked through his mind then: he was black with rock dust—would he have time to wash before donning the white tunic of candidacy? And if the eggs were hatching, why hadn't the candidates been recalled by the wingsecond?

"Naw! Guess again!" Beterli was much too pleased with himself.

With a sinking heart, Keevan knew what the news must be, and he could only stare with intense desolation at the older boy.

"C'mon! Guess, babe!"

"I've no time for guessing games," Keevan managed to say with indifference. He began to shovel black rock into the barrow as fast as he could.

"I said guess." Beterli grabbed the shovel.

"And I said I have no time for guessing games."

Beterli wrenched the shovel from Keevan's hands.

"I'll have that shovel back, Beterli." Keevan straightened up but he didn't come to Beterli's bulky shoulder. From somewhere, other boys appeared, some with barrows, some mysteriously alerted to the prospect of a confrontation among their numbers.

"Babes don't give orders to candidates around here, babe!"

Someone sniggered and Keevan, incredulous, knew that he must've been dropped from the candidacy.

He yanked the shovel from Beterli's loosened grasp. Snarling, the older boy tried to regain possession, but Keevan clung with all his strength to the handle, dragged back and forth as the stronger boy jerked the shovel about.

With a sudden, unexpected movement, Beterli rammed the handle into Keevan's chest, knocking him over the barrow handles. Keevan felt a sharp, painful jab behind his left ear, an unbearable pain in his left shin, and then a painless nothingness.

Mende's angry voice roused him, and startled, he tried to throw back the covers, thinking he'd overslept. But he

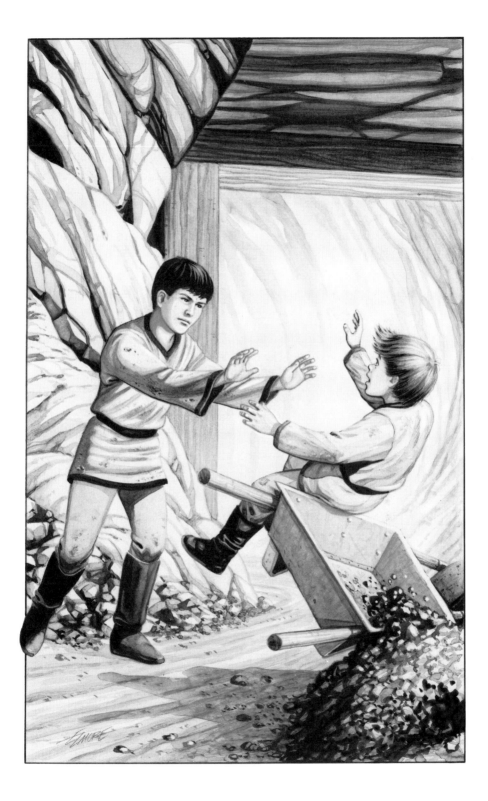

couldn't move, so firmly was he tucked into his bed. And then the constriction of a bandage on his head and the dull sickishness in his leg brought back recent occurrences.

"Hatching?" he cried.

"No, lovey," Mende said in a kind voice. Her hand was cool and gentle on his forehead. "Though there's some as won't be at any hatching again." Her voice took on a stern edge.

Keevan looked beyond her to see the Weyrwoman, who was frowning with irritation.

"Keevan, will you tell me what occurred at the black rock bunker?" asked Lessa in an even voice.

He remembered Beterli now and the quarrel over the shovel and . . . what had Mende said about some not being at any hatching? Much as he hated Beterli, he couldn't bring himself to tattle on Beterli and force him out of candidacy.

"Come, lad," and a note of impatience crept into the Weyrwoman's voice. "I merely want to know what happened from you, too. Mende said she sent you for black rock. Beterli—and every Weyrling in the cavern—seems to have been on the same errand. What happened?"

"Beterli took my shovel. I hadn't finished with it."

"There's more than one shovel. What did he *say* to you?"

"He'd heard the news."

"What news?" The Weyrwoman was suddenly amused.

"That . . . that . . . there'd been changes."

"Is that what he said?"

"Not exactly."

"What did he say? C'mon, lad, I've heard from everyone else, you know."

"He said for me to guess the news."

"And you fell for that old gag?" The Weyrwoman's irritation returned.

"Consider all the talk last night at supper, Lessa," Mende said. "Of course the boy would think he'd been eliminated."

"In effect, he is, with a broken skull and leg." Lessa touched his arm in a rare gesture of sympathy. "Be that as it may, Keevan, you'll have other Impressions. Beterli will not. There are certain rules that must be observed by all candidates, and his conduct proves him unacceptable to the Weyr."

She smiled at Mende and then left.

"I'm still a candidate?" Keevan asked urgently.

"Well, you are and you aren't, lovey," his foster mother said. "Is the numbweed working?" she asked, and when he nodded, she said, "You must rest. I'll bring you some nice broth."

At any other time in his life, Keevan would have relished such cosseting, but now he just lay there worrying. Beterli had been dismissed. Would the others think it was his fault? But everyone was there! Beterli provoked that fight. His worry increased, because although he heard excited comings and goings in the passageway, no one tweaked back the curtain across the sleeping alcove he shared with five other boys. Surely one of them would have to come in sometime. No, they were all avoiding him. And something else was wrong. Only he didn't know what.

Mende returned with broth and beachberry bread.

"Why doesn't anyone come see me, Mende? I haven't done anything wrong, have I? I didn't ask to have Beterli turfed out."

Mende soothed him, saying everyone was busy with noon-time chores and no one was angry with him. They were giving him a chance to rest in quiet. The numbweed made him drowsy, and her words were fair enough. He permitted his fears to dissipate. Until he heard a hum. Actually, he felt it first, in the broken shin bone and his sore head. The hum began to grow. Two things registered suddenly in Keevan's groggy mind: the only white candidate's robe still on the pegs in the chamber was his; and the dragons hummed when a clutch was being laid or being hatched. Impression! And he was flat abed.

Bitter, bitter disappointment turned the warm broth sour in his belly. Even the small voice telling him that he'd have other opportunities failed to alleviate his crushing depression. *This* was the Impression that mattered! This was his chance to show *everyone,* from Mende to K'last to L'vel and even the Weyrleader, that he, Keevan, was worthy of being a dragonrider.

He twisted in bed, fighting against the tears that threatened to choke him. Dragonmen don't cry! Dragonmen learn to live with pain.

Pain? The leg didn't actually pain him as he rolled about on his bedding. His head felt sort of stiff from the tightness of the bandage. He sat up, an effort in itself since the numbweed made exertion difficult. He touched the splintered leg; the knee was unhampered. He had no feeling in his bone, really. He swung himself carefully to the side of his bed and stood slowly. The room wanted to swim about him. He closed his eyes, which made the dizziness worse, and he had to clutch the wall.

Gingerly, he took a step. The broken leg dragged. It hurt in spite of the numbweed, but what was pain to a dragonman?

No one had said he couldn't go to the Impression. "You are and you aren't" were Mende's exact words.

Clinging to the wall, he jerked off his bedshirt. Stretching his arm to the utmost, he jerked his white candidate's tunic from the peg. Jamming first one arm and then the other into the holes, he pulled it over his head. Too bad about the belt. He couldn't wait. He hobbled to the door, hung on to the curtain to steady himself. The weight on his leg was unwieldy. He wouldn't get very far without something to lean on. Down by the bathing pool was one of the long crook-necked poles used to retrieve clothes from the hot troughs. But it was down there, and he was on the level above. And there was no one nearby to come to his aid: everyone would be in the Hatching Ground right now, eagerly waiting for the first egg to crack.

The humming increased in volume and tempo, an urgency to which Keevan responded, knowing that his time was all too limited if he was to join the ranks of the hopeful boys standing around the cracking eggs. But if he hurried down the ramp, he'd fall flat on his face.

He could, of course, go flat on his rear end, the way crawling children did. He sat down, sending a jarring stab of pain through his leg and up to the wound on the back of his head. Gritting his teeth and blinking away tears, Keevan scrabbled down the ramp. He had to wait a moment at the bottom to catch his breath. He got to one knee, the injured leg straight out in front of him. Somehow he managed to push himself erect, though the room seemed about to tip over his ears. It wasn't far to the crooked stick, but it seemed an age before he had it in his hand.

Then the humming stopped!

Keevan cried out and began to hobble frantically across the cavern, out to the bowl of the Weyr. Never had the distance between living caverns and the Hatching Ground seemed so great. Never had the Weyr been so breathlessly silent. It was as if the multitude of people and dragons watching the hatching held every breath in suspense. Not even the wind muttered down the steep sides of the bowl. The only sounds to break the stillness were Keevan's ragged gasps and the thump-thud of his stick on the hard-packed ground. Sometimes he had to hop twice on his good leg to maintain his balance. Twice he fell into the sand and had to pull himself up on the stick, his white tunic no longer spotless. Once he jarred himself so badly he couldn't get up immediately.

Then he heard the first exhalation of the crowd, the oohs, the muted cheer, the susurrus of excited whispers. An egg had cracked, and the dragon had chosen his rider. Desperation increased Keevan's hobble. Would he never reach the arching mouth of the Hatching Ground?

Another cheer and an excited spate of applause spurred Keevan to greater effort. If he didn't get there in moments, there'd be no unpaired hatchling left. Then he was actually staggering into the Hatching Ground, the sands hot on his bare feet.

No one noticed his entrance or his halting progress. And Keevan could see nothing but the backs of the white-robed candidates, seventy of them ringing the area around the egg. Then one side would surge forward or back and there'd be a cheer. Another dragon had been Impressed. Suddenly a large gap appeared in the white human wall, and Keevan had his first sight of the eggs. There didn't seem to be *any* left uncracked, and he could see the lucky boys standing beside wobble-legged dragons. He could hear the unmistakable plaintive crooning of hatchlings and their squawks of protest as they'd fall awkwardly in the sand.

Suddenly he wished that he hadn't left his bed, that he'd stayed away from the Hatching Ground. Now everyone would see his ignominious failure. So he scrambled as desperately to reach the shadowy walls of the Hatching Ground as he struggled to cross the bowl. He mustn't be seen.

He didn't notice, therefore, that the shifting group of boys remaining had begun to drift in his direction. The hard pace he had set himself and his cruel disappointment took their double toll of Keevan. He tripped and collapsed sobbing to the warm sands. He didn't see the consternation in the watching Weyrfolk above the Hatching Ground, nor did he hear the excited whispers of speculation. He didn't know that the Weyrleader and Weyrwoman had dropped to the arena and were making their way toward the knot of boys slowly moving in the direction of the entrance.

"Never seen anything like it," the Weyrleader was saying. "Only thirty-nine riders chosen. And the bronze trying to leave the Hatching Ground without making Impression."

"A case in point of what I said last night," the Weyrwoman replied, "where a hatchling makes no choice because the right boy isn't there."

"There's only Beterli and K'last's young one missing. And there's a full wing of likely boys to choose from . . ."

"None acceptable, apparently. Where is the creature going? He's not heading for the entrance after all. Oh, what have we there, in the shadows?"

Keevan heard with dismay the sound of voices nearing him. He tried to burrow into the sand. The mere thought of how he would be teased and taunted now was unbearable.

Don't worry! Please don't worry! The thought was urgent, but not his own.

Someone kicked sand over Keevan and butted roughly against him.

"Go away. Leave me alone!" he cried.

Why? was the injured-sounding question inserted into his mind. There was no voice, no tone, but the question was there, perfectly clear, in his head.

Incredulous, Keevan lifted his head and stared into the glowing jeweled eyes of a small bronze dragon. His wings were wet, the tips drooping in the sand. And he sagged in the middle on his unsteady legs, although he was making a great effort to keep erect.

Keevan dragged himself to his knees, oblivious of the pain in his leg. He wasn't even aware that he was ringed by the boys passed over, while thirty-one pairs of resentful eyes watched him Impress the dragon. The Weyrmen looked on, amused, and surprised at the draconic choice, which could not be forced. Could not be questioned. Could not be changed.

Why? asked the dragon again. *Don't you like me?* His eyes whirled with anxiety, and his tone was so piteous that Keevan staggered forward and threw his arms around the dragon's neck, stroking his eye ridges, patting the damp, soft hide, opening the fragile-looking wings to dry them, and wordlessly assuring the hatchling over and over again that he was the most perfect, most beautiful, most beloved dragon in the Weyr, in all the Weyrs of Pern.

"What's his name, K'van?" asked Lessa, smiling warmly at the new dragonrider. K'van stared up at her for a long moment. Lessa would know as soon as he did. Lessa was the only person who could "receive" from all dragons, not only her own Ramoth. Then he gave her a radiant smile, recognizing the traditional shortening of his name that raised him forever to the rank of dragonrider.

My name is Heth, the dragon thought mildly, then hiccuped in sudden urgency. *I'm hungry.*

"Dragons are born hungry," said Lessa, laughing. "F'lar, give the boy a hand. He can barely manage his own legs, much less a dragon's."

K'van remembered his stick and drew himself up. "We'll be just fine, thank you."

"You may be the smallest dragonrider ever, young K'van," F'lar said, "but you're one of the bravest!"

And Heth agreed! Pride and joy so leaped in both chests

that K'van wondered if his heart would burst right out of his body. He looped an arm around Heth's neck and the pair, the smallest dragonboy and the hatchling who wouldn't choose anybody else, walked out of the Hatching Ground together forever.

A Message from Charity

William Lee

THAT SUMMER of the year 1700 was the hottest in the memory of the very oldest inhabitants. Because the year ushered in a new century, some held that the events were related and that for a whole hundred years Bay Colony would be as torrid and steamy as the Indies themselves.

There was a good deal of illness in Annes Towne, and a score had died before the weather broke at last in late September. For the great part they were oldsters who succumbed, but some of the young were sick too, and Charity Payne as sick as any.

Charity had turned eleven in the spring and had still the figure and many of the ways of thinking of a child, but she was tall and strong and tanned by the New England sun, for she spent many hours helping her father in the fields and trying to keep some sort of order in the dooryard and garden.

During the weeks when she lay bedridden and, for a time, burning up with fever, Thomas Carter and his good wife Beulah came as neighbors should to lend a hand, for Charity's mother had died abirthing and Obie Payne could not cope all alone.

Charity lay on a pallet covered by a straw-filled mattress which her father, frantic to be doing something for her and finding little enough to do beyond the saying of short fervent prayers, refilled with fresh straw as often as Beulah would allow. A few miles down Harmon Brook was a famous beaver pond where in winter the Annes Towne people cut ice to be stored under layers of bark and chips. It had been used heavily early in the summer, and there was not very much ice left, but those families with sickness in the home might draw upon it for the patient's comfort. So Charity had bits of ice folded into a woolen cloth to lay on her forehead when the fever was bad.

William Trowbridge, who had apprenticed in medicine down in Philadelphia, attended the girl, and pronounced her illness a sort of summer cholera which was claiming victims all up and down the brook. Trowbridge was only moderately esteemed in Annes Towne, being better, it was said, at delivering lambs and foals than at treating human maladies. He was a gruff and notional man, and he was prone to state his views on a subject and then walk away instead of waiting to argue and perhaps be refuted. Not easy to get along with.

For Charity he prescribed a diet of beef tea with barley and another tea, very unpleasant to the taste, made from pounded willow bark. What was more, all her drinking water was to be boiled. Since there was no other advice to be had, they followed it and in due course Charity got well.

She ran a great fever for five days, and it was midway in this period when the strange dreams began. Not dreams really, for she was awake though often out of her senses, knowing her father now and then, other times seeing him as a gaunt and frightening stranger. When she was better, still weak but wholly rational, she tried to tell her visitors about these dreams.

"Some person was talking and talking," she recalled. "A man or perchance a lad. He talked not to me, but I could hear or understand all that he said. 'Twas strange talk indeed, a porridge of the King's English and other words of no sense at all. And with the talk I did see some fearful sights."

"La, now, don't even think of it," said Dame Beulah.

"But I would fen both think and talk of it, for I am no longer afeared. Such things I saw in bits and flashes, as 'twere seen by a strike of lightning."

"Talk and ye be so minded, then. There's naught impious in y'r conceits. Tell me again about the carriages which traneled along with nary horse."

Annes Towne survived the Revolution and the War of 1812, and for a time seemed likely to become a larger, if not an important community. But when its farms became less productive and the last virgin timber disappeared from the area, Annes Towne began to disappear too, dwindling from two score of homes to a handful, then to none; and the last foundation had crumbled to rubble and been scattered a hundred years before it could have been nominated a historic site.

In time dirt tracks became stone roads, which gave way to black meanderings of macadam, and these in their turn were displaced by never ending bands of concrete. The cross-roads site of Annes Towne was presently cleared of brambles, sumac and red cedar, and overnight it was a shopping center. Now, for mile on spreading mile the New England hills were dotted with ranch houses, salt boxes and split-level colonial homes.

During four decades Harmon Brook had been fouled and poisoned by a textile bleach and dye works. Rising labor costs had at last driven the small company to extinction. With that event and increasingly rigorous legislation, the stream had come back to the extent that it could now be bordered by some of these prosperous homes and by the golf course of the Anniston Country Club.

With aquatic plants and bullfrogs and a few fish inhabiting its waters, it was not obvious to implicate the Harmon for the small outbreak of typhoid which occurred in the hot dry summer of 1965. No one was dependent on it for drinking water. To the discomfort of a local milk distributor, who was entirely blameless, indictment of the stream was delayed and obscured by the fact that the organisms involved were not a typical strain of *Salmonella typhosa*. Indeed they ultimately found a place in the American Type Culture Collection, under a new number.

Young Peter Wood, whose home was one of those pleasantly situated along the stream, was the most seriously ill of all the cases, partly because he was the first, mostly because his symptoms went unremarked for a time. Peter was sixteen and not highly communicative to either parents or friends. The Wood Seniors both taught, at Harvard and Wellesley respectively. They were intelligent and well-intentioned parents, but sometimes a little off-hand, and like many of their friends, they raised their son to be a miniature adult in as many ways as possible. His sports, tennis and golf, were adult sports. His reading tastes were catholic, ranging from Camus to Al Capp to science fiction. He had been carefully held back in his progress through the lower grades so that he would not enter college more than a year or so ahead of his age. He had an adequate number of friends and sufficient areas of congeniality with them. He had gotten a driver's license shortly after his sixteenth birthday and drove seriously and well enough to be allowed nearly unrestricted use of the second car.

So Peter Wood was not the sort of boy to complain to his family about headache, mild nausea and other symptoms. Instead, after they had persisted for forty-eight hours, he telephoned for an appointment on his own initiative and visited the family doctor. Suddenly, in the waiting room, he became much worse, and was given a cot in an examining room until Dr. Maxwell was free to drive him home. The doctor did not seriously suspect typhoid, though it was among several possibilities which he counted as less likely.

Peter's temperature rose from 104 degrees to over 105 degrees that night. No nurse was to be had until morning, and his parents alternated in attendance in his bedroom. There was no cause for alarm, since the patient was full of wide-spectrum antibiotic. But he slept only fitfully with intervals of waking delirium. He slapped at the sheet, tossed around on the bed and muttered or spoke now and then. Some of the talk was understandable.

"There's a forest," he said.

"What?" asked his father.

"There's a forest the other side of the stream."

"Oh."

"Can you see it?"

"No, I'm sitting inside here with you. Take it easy, son."

"Some deer are coming down to drink, along the edge of Weller's pasture."

"Is that so?"

"Last year a mountain lion killed two of them, right where they drank. Is it raining?"

"No, it isn't. It would be fine if we could have some."

"It's raining. I can hear it on the roof." A pause. "It drips down the chimney."

Peter turned his head to look at his father, momentarily clear-eyed.

"How long since there's been a forest across the stream?"

Dr. Wood reflected on the usual difficulty of answering explicit questions and on his own ignorance of history.

"A long time. I expect this valley has been farmland since colonial days."

"Funny." Peter said. "I shut my eyes and I can see a forest. Really big trees. On our side of the stream there's a kind of a garden and an apple tree and a path goes down to the water."

"It sounds pleasant."

"Yeah."

"Why don't you try going to sleep?"

"Okay."

The antibiotic accomplished much less than it should have done in Peter's case, and he stayed very sick for several days. Even after diagnosis, there appeared no good reason to move him from home. A trained nurse was on duty after that first night, and tranquilizers and sedatives reduced her job to no more than keeping a watch. There were only a few sleepy communications from her young patient. It was on the fourth night, the last one when he had any significant fever, that he asked.

"Were you ever a girl?"

"Well, thanks a lot. I'm not as old as all that."

"I mean, were you ever inside a girl?"

"I think you'd better go back to sleep, young man."

He uttered no oddities thereafter, at least when there was anyone within hearing. During the days of his recovery and convalescence, abed and later stretched out on a chaise longue on the terrace looking down toward Harmon Brook, he took to whispering. He moved his lips hardly at all, but vocalized each word, or if he fell short of this, at least put each thought into carefully chosen words and sentences.

The idea that he might be in mental communication with another person was not, to him, very startling. Steeped in the lore of science fiction whose heroes were, as like as not, adepts at telepathy, the event seemed almost an expected outcome of his wishes. Many nights he had lain awake sending out (he hoped) a mental probe, trying and trying to find the trick, for surely there must be one, of making a contact.

Now that such a contact was established he sought, just as vainly, for some means to prove it. How do you know you're not dreaming, he asked himself. How do you know you're not still delirious?

The difficulty was that his communication with Charity Payne could be by mental route only. Had there been any possibility for Peter to reach the girl by mail, by telephone, by travel and a personal visit, their rapport on a mental level might have been confirmed, and their messages cross-checked.

During their respective periods of illness, Peter and Charity achieved a communion of a sort which consisted at first of brief glimpses, each of the other's environment. They were not—then—seeing through one another's eyes, so much as tapping one another's visual recollections. While Peter stared at a smoothly plastered ceiling, Charity looked at rough-hewn beams. He, when his aching head permitted, could turn on one side and watch a television program. She, by the same movement, could see a small smoky fire in the monstrous stone fireplace, where water was heated and her beef and barley broth kept steaming.

Instead of these current images, current for each of them in their different times, they saw stored-up pictures, not perfect, for neither of them was remembering perfectly; rather like pictures viewed through a badly ground lens, with only the objects of principal interest in clear detail.

Charity saw her fearful sights with no basis for comprehension—a section of dual highway animated by hurtling cars and trucks and not a person, recognizable as a person, in sight; a tennis court, and what on earth could it be; a jet plane crossing the sky; a vast and many-storied building which glinted with glass and the silvery tracings of untarnished steel.

At the start she was terrified nearly out of her wits. It's all very well to dream, and a nightmare is only a bad dream after you waken, but a nightmare is assembled from familiar props. You could reasonably be chased by a dragon (like the one in the picture that St. George had to fight) or be lost in a cave (like the one on Parish Hill, only bigger and darker). To dream of things which have no meaning at all is worse.

She was spared prolongation of her terror by Peter's comprehension of their situation and his intuitive realization of what the experience, assuming a two-way channel might be doing to her. The vignettes of her life which he was seeing were in no way disturbing. Everything he saw through her mind was within his framework of reference. Horses and cattle, fields and forest, rutted lanes and narrow wooden bridges were things he knew, even if he did not live among them. He recognized Harmon Brook because, directly below their home, there was an immense granite boulder parting the flow, shaped like a great bearlike animal with its head down, drinking. It was strange that the stream, in all those years, had neither silted up nor eroded away to hide or change the seeming of the rock, but so it was. He saw it through Charity's eyes and knew the place in spite of the forest on the far hill.

When he first saw this partly familiar, partly strange scene, he heard from somewhere within his mind the frightened cry of a little girl. His thinking at that time was fever-distorted and incoherent. It was two days later after a period of several hours of normal temperature when he conceived the idea—with sudden virtual certainty—these pastoral scenes he had been dreaming were truly something seen with other eyes. There were subtle perceptual differences between those pictures and his own seeing.

To his mother, writing at a table near the windows, he said, "I think I'm feeling better. How about a glass of orange juice?"

She considered. "The doctor should be here in an hour or so. In the meantime you can make do with a little more ice water. I'll get it. Drink it slowly, remember."

Two hundred and sixty-five years away, Charity Payne thought suddenly, "How about a glass of orange juice?" She had been drowsing, but her eyes popped wide open. "Mercy," she said aloud. Dame Beulah bent over the pallet.

"What is it, child?"

"How about a glass of orange juice?" Charity repeated.

"La, 'tis gibberish." A cool hand was laid on her forehead. "Would ye like a bit of ice to bite on?"

Orange juice, whatever that might be, was forgotten.

Over the next several days Peter Wood tried time and again to address the stranger directly, and repeatedly failed. Some of what he said to others reached her in fragments and further confused her state of mind. What she had to say, on the other hand, was coming through to him with increasing frequency. Often it was only a word or a phrase with a quaint twist like a historical novel, and he would lie puzzling over it, trying to place the person on the other end of their erratic line of communication. His recognition of Bear Rock, which he had seen once again through her eyes, was disturbing. His science fiction conditioning led him naturally to speculate about the parallel worlds concept, but that seemed not to fit the facts as he saw them.

Peter reached the stage of convalescence when he could spend all day on the terrace and look down, when he wished, at the actual rock. There for the hundredth time he formed the syllables, "Hello, who are you?" and for the first time received a response. It was a silence, but a silence reverberating with shock, totally different in quality from the blankness which had met him before.

"My name is Peter Wood."

There was a long pause before the answer came, softly and timidly.

"My name is Charity Payne. Where are you? What is happening to me?"

The following days of enforced physical idleness were filled with exploration and discovery. Peter found out almost at once that, while they were probably no more than a few feet apart in their respective worlds, a gulf of more than a quarter of a thousand years stretched between them. Such a contact through time was a greater departure from known physical laws, certainly, than the mere fact of telepathic communication. Peter reveled in his growing ability.

In another way the situation was heartbreaking. No matter how well they came to know one another, he realized, they could never meet, and after no more than a few hours of acquaintance he found that he was regarding this naïve child of another time with esteem and a sort of affection.

They arrived shortly at a set of rules which seemed to govern and limit their communications. Each came to be able to hear the other speak, whether aloud or subvocally. Each learned to perceive through the other's senses, up to a point. Visual perception became better and better especially for direct seeing while, as they grew more skillful, the remembered scene became less clear. Tastes and odors could be transmitted, if not accurately, at least with the expected response. Tactile sensations could not be perceived in the slightest degree.

There was little that Peter Wood could learn from Charity. He came to recognize her immediate associates and liked them, particularly her gaunt, weatherbeaten father. He formed a picture of Puritanism which, as an ethic, he had to respect, while the supporting dogma evoked nothing but impatience. At first he exposed her to the somewhat scholarly agnosticism which prevailed in his own home, but soon found that it distressed her deeply and he left off. There was so much he could report from the vantage of 1965, so many things he would show her which did not conflict with her tenets and faith.

He discovered that Charity's ability to read was remarkable, though what she had read was naturally limited—the Bible from cover to cover, *Pilgrim's Progress,* several essays and two of Shakespeare's plays. Encouraged by a schoolmaster who must have been an able and dedicated man, she had read and reread everything permitted to her. Her quite respectable vocabulary was gleaned from these sources and may have equaled Peter's own in size. In addition she possessed an uncanny word sense which helped her greatly in understanding Peter's jargon.

She learned the taste of bananas and frankfurters, chocolate ice cream and Coke, and displayed such an addiction to these delicacies that Peter rapidly put on some of the pounds he had lost. One day she asked him what he looked like.

"Well, I told you I am sixteen, and I'm sort of thin."

"Does thee possess a mirror?" she asked.

"Yes, of course."

At her urging and with some embarrassment he went and stood before a mirrored door in his mother's bedroom.

"Marry," she said after a dubious pause, "I doubt not thee is comely. But folk have changed."

"Now let me look at you," he demanded.

"Nay, we have no mirror."

"Then go and look in the brook. There's a quiet spot below the rock where the water is dark."

He was delighted with her appearance, having remembered Hogarth's unkind representations of a not much later period and being prepared for disappointment. She was in fact very much prettier by Peter's standards than by those of her own time, which favored plumpness and smaller mouths. He told her she was a beauty, and her tentative fondness for him turned instantly to adulation.

Previously Peter had had fleeting glimpses of her slim, smoothly muscled body, as she had bathed or dressed. Now, having seen each other face-to-face, they were overcome by embarrassment and both of them, when not fully clothed, stared resolutely into the corners of the room.

For a time Charity believed that Peter was a dreadful liar. The sight and sound of planes in the sky were not enough to convince her of the fact of flying, so he persuaded his father to take him along on a business flight to Washington. After she had recovered from the marvels of airplane travel, he took her on a walking tour of the Capitol. Now she would believe anything, even that the American Revolution had been a success. They joined his father for lunch at an elegant French restaurant and she experienced, vicariously, the pleasures of half of a half bottle of white wine and a chocolate eclair. Charity was by way of getting spoiled.

Fully recovered and with school only a week away, Peter decided to brush up on his tennis. When reading or doing nothing in particular, he was always dimly aware of Charity and her immediate surroundings, and by sharpening his attention he could bring her clearly to the forefront of his mind. Tennis displaced her completely and for an hour or two each day he was unaware of her doings.

Had he been a few years older and a little more knowledgeable and realistic about the world, he might have guessed the peril into which he was leading her. Fictional villainy abounded, of course, and many items in the news didn't bear thinking about, but by his own firsthand experience, people were well intentioned and kindly, and for the most part they reacted to events with reasonable intelligence. It was what he expected instinctively.

A first hint of possible consequences reached him as he walked home from one of his tennis sessions.

"Ursula Miller said an ill thing to me today."

"Oh?" His answer was abstracted since, in all truth, he was beginning to run out of interest in the village gossip which was all the news she had to offer.

"Yesterday she said it was an untruth about the thirteen states. Today she avowed that I was devil-ridden. And Ursula has been my best friend."

"I warned you that people wouldn't believe you and you might get yourself laughed at," he said. Then suddenly he caught up in his thinking. "Good Lord—Salem."

"Please, Peter, thee must stop taking thy Maker's name."

"I'll try to remember. Listen, Charity, how many people have you been talking to about our—about what's been happening?"

"As I have said. At first to Father and Aunt Beulah. They did believe I was still addled from the fever."

"And to Ursula."

"Aye, but she vowed to keep it secret."

"Do you believe she will, now that she's started name-calling?"

A lengthy pause.

"I fear she may have told the lad who keeps her company."

"I should have warned you. Damn it, I should have laid it on the line."

"Peter!"

"Sorry. Charity, not another word to anybody. Tell Ursula you've been fooling—telling stories to amuse her."

" 'Twould not be right."

"So what. Charity, don't be scared, but listen. People might get to thinking you're a witch."

"Oh, they couldn't."

"Why not?"

"Because I am not one. Witches are—oh, no, Peter."

He could sense her growing alarm.

"Go tell Ursula it was a pack of lies. Do it now."

"I must milk the cow."

"Do it now."

"Nay, the cow must be milked."

"Then milk her faster than she's ever been milked before."

On the Sabbath, three little boys threw stones at Charity as she and her father left the church. Obadiah Payne caught one of them and caned him, and then would have had to fight the lad's father save that the pastor intervened.

It was on the Wednesday that calamity befell. Two tight-lipped men approached Obadiah in the fields.

"Squire wants to see thy daughter Charity."

"Squire?"

"Aye. Squire Hacker. He would talk with her at once."

"Squire can talk to me if so be he would have her reprimanded. What has she been up to?"

"Witchcraft, that's what," said the second man, sounding as if he were savoring the dread news. "Croft's old ewe delivered a monstrous lamb. Pointy pinched-up face and an extra eye." He crossed himself.

"Great God!"

" 'Twill do ye no good to blaspheme, Obadiah. She's to come with us now."

"I'll not have it. Charity's no witch, as ye well know, and I'll not have her converse with Squire. Ye mind the Squire's lecherous ways."

"That's not here nor there. Witchcraft is afoot again and all are saying 'tis your Charity at bottom of it."

"She shall not go."

First one, then the other displayed the stout truncheons they had held concealed behind their backs.

" 'Twas of our own good will we told thee first. Come now and instruct thy daughter to go with us featly. Else take a clout on the head and sleep tonight in the gaol house."

They left Obie Payne gripping a broken wrist and staring in numbed bewilderment from his door stoop, and escorted Charity, not touching her, walking at a cautious distance to either side, to Squire Hacker's big house on the hill. In the village proper, little groups of people watched from doorways and, though some had always been her good friends, none had the courage now to speak a word of comfort.

Peter went with her each reluctant step of the way, counting himself responsible for her plight and helpless to do the least thing about it. He sat alone in the living room of his home, eyes closed to sharpen his reading of her surroundings. She offered no response to his whispered reassurances and perhaps did not hear them.

At the door her guards halted and stood aside, leaving her face-to-face with the grim-visaged squire. He moved backward step by step, and she followed him, as if hypnotized, into the shadowed room.

The squire lowered himself into a high-backed chair. "Look at me."

Unwillingly she raised her head and stared into his face.

Squire Hacker was a man of medium height, very broad in the shoulder and heavily muscled. His face was disfigured by deep pockmarks and the scar of a knife cut across the jaw, souvenirs of his earlier years in the Carib Islands. From the Islands he had also brought some wealth which he had since increased manyfold by the buying of land, sharecropping and moneylending.

"Charity Payne," he said sternly, "take off thy frock."

"No. No, please."

"I command it. Take off thy garments, for I must search thee for witch marks."

He leaned forward, seized her arm and pulled her to him. "If thee would avoid public trial and condemnation, thee will do as I say." His hands began to explore her body.

Even by the standards of the time, Charity regularly spent extraordinary hours at hard physical labor and she possessed a strength which would have done credit to many young men. Squire Hacker should have been more cautious.

"Nay," she shouted and, drawing back her arm, hit him in the nose with all the force she could muster. He released her with a roar of rage, then, while he was mopping away blood and tears with the sleeve of his ruffled shirt and shouting imprecations, she turned and shot out the door. The guards, converging, nearly grabbed her as she passed but, once away, they stood no chance of catching her and for a wonder none of the villagers took up the chase.

She was well on the way home and covering the empty road at a fast trot before Peter was able to gain her attention.

"Charity," he said. "Charity, you mustn't go home. If that s.o.b. of a squire has any influence with the court, you just fixed yourself."

She was beginning to think again and could even translate Peter's strange language.

"Influence!" she said. "Marry, he is the court. He is the judge."

"Ouch!"

"I wot well I must not be found at home. I am trying to think where to hide. I might have had trial by water. Now they will burn me for surety. I do remember what folk said about the last witch trials."

"Could you make your way to Boston and then maybe to New York-New Amsterdam?"

"Leave my home forever! Nay. And I would not dare the trip."

"Then take to the woods. Where can you go?"

"Take to—? Oh. To the cave, mayhap."

"Don't too many people know about it?"

"Aye. But there is another across the brook and beyond Tom Carter's freehold. I do believe none know of it but me. 'Tis very small. We must ford the brook just yonder, then walk that fallen tree. There is a trail which at sundown will be tromped by a herd of deer."

"You're thinking about dogs?"

"Aye, on the morrow. There is no good pack in Annes Towne."

"You live in a savage age, Charity."

"Aye," she said wryly. " 'Tis fortunate we have not invented the bomb."

"Damn it," Peter said. "I wish we'd never met. I wish I hadn't taken you on the plane trip. I wish I'd warned you to keep quiet about it."

"Ye could not guess I would be so foolish."

"What can you do out here without food?"

"I'd liefer starve than be in the stocks, but there is food to be had in the forest, some sorts of roots and toadstools and autumn berries. I shall hide myself for three days, I think, then seek out my father by night and do as he tells me."

When she was safely hidden in the cave, which was small indeed but well concealed by a thicket of young sassafras, she said:

"Now we can think. First, I would have an answer from thy

• 37

superior wisdom. Can one be truly a witch and have no knowledge of it?"

"Don't be foolish. There's no such thing as a witch."

"Ah well, 'tis a matter for debate by scholars. I do feel in my heart that I am not a witch, if there be such creatures. That book, Peter, of which ye told me, which recounts the history of these colonies."

"Yes?"

"Will ye look in it and learn if I came to trial and what befell me?"

"There'd be nothing about it. It's just a small book. But—"

To his parents' puzzlement, Peter spent the following morning at the Boston Public Library. In the afternoon he shifted his operations to the Historical Society. He found at last a listing of the names of women known to have been tried for witchcraft between the years 1692 and 1697. Thereafter he could locate only an occasional individual name. There was no record of any Charity Payne in 1700 or later.

He started again when the reading room opened next day, interrupting the task only momentarily for brief exchanges with Charity. His lack of success was cheering to her, for she overestimated the completeness of the records.

At close to noon he was scanning the pages of a photostated doctoral thesis when his eye caught a familiar name.

Jonas Hacker, born Liverpool, England, date uncertain, perhaps 1659, was the principal figure in a curious action of law which has not become a recognized legal precedent in English courts.

Squire Hacker, a resident of Annes Towne (cf. Anniston), was tried and convicted of willful murder and larceny. The trial was posthumous, several months after his decease from natural causes in 1704. The sentence pronounced was death by hanging which, since it could not be imposed, was commuted to forfeiture of his considerable estate. His land and other possessions reverted to the Crown and were henceforward administered by the Governor of Bay Colony.

While the motivation and procedure of the court may have been open to question, evidence of Hacker's guilt was clear-cut. The details are these . . .

"Hey, Charity," Peter rumbled in his throat.

"Aye?"

"Look at this page. Let me flatten it out."

"Read it please, Peter. Is it bad news?"

"No. Good, I think." He read the paragraphs on Jonas Hacker.

"Oh, Peter, can it be true?"

"It has to be. Can you remember any details?"

"Marry, I remember well when they disappeared, the ship's captain and a common sailor. They were said to have a great sack of gold for some matter of business with Squire. But it could not be, for they never reached his house."

"That's what Hacker said, but the evidence showed that they got there—got there and never got away. Now here's what you must do. Late tonight, go home."

"I would fen do so, for I am terrible athirst."

"No, wait. What's your parson's name?"

"John Hix."

"Can you reach his house tonight without being seen?"

"Aye. It backs on a glen."

"Go there. He can protect you better than your father can until your trial."

"Must I be tried?"

"Of course. We want to clear your name. Now let's do some planning."

The town hall could seat no more than a score of people, and the day was fair; so it was decided that the trial should be held on the common, in discomforting proximity to the stocks.

Visitors came from as far as twenty miles away, afoot or in carts, and nearly filled the common itself. Squire Hacker's own armchair was the only seat provided. Others stood or sat on the patchy grass.

The squire came out of the inn presently, fortified with rum, and took his place. He wore a brocaded coat and a wide-brimmed hat and would have been more impressive if it had not been for his still swollen nose, now permanently askew.

A way was made through the crowd then, and Charity, flanked on one side by John Hix, on the other by his tall son, walked to the place where she was to stand. Voices were suddenly stilled. Squire Hacker did not condescend to look directly at the prisoner, but fixed a cold stare on the minister: a warning that his protection of the girl would not be forgiven. He cleared his throat.

"Charity Payne, is thee willing to swear upon the Book?"

"Aye."

"No mind. We may forego the swearing. All can see that ye are fearful."

"Nay," John Hix interrupted. "She shall have the opportunity to swear to her word. 'Twould not be legal otherwise." He extended a Bible to Charity, who placed her fingers on it and said, "I do swear to speak naught but the truth."

Squire Hacker glowered and lost no time coming to the attack. "Charity Payne, do ye deny being a witch?"

"I do."

"Ye do be one?"

"Nay, I do deny it."

"Speak what ye mean. What have ye to say of the monstrous lamb born of Master Croft's ewe?"

"I know naught of it."

"Was't the work of Satan?"

"I know not."

"Was't then the work of God?"

"I know not."

"Thee holds then that He might create such a monster?"

"I know naught about it."

"In thy own behalf will thee deny saying that this colony and its neighbors will in due course make wars against our King?"

"Nay, I do not deny that."

There was a stir in the crowd and some angry muttering.

"Did ye tell Mistress Ursula Miller that ye had flown a great journey through the air?"

"Nay."

"Mistress Ursula will confound thee in that lie."

"I did tell Ursula that someday folk would travel in that wise. I did tell her that I had seen such travel through eyes other than my own."

Squire Hacker leaned forward. He could not have hoped for a more damning statement. John Hix's head bowed in prayer.

"Continue."

"Aye. I am blessed with a sort of second sight."

"Blessed or cursed?"

"God permits it. It cannot be accursed."

"Continue. What evil things do ye see by this second sight?"

"Most oftentimes I see the world as it will one day be.

42 •

Thee said evil. Such sights are no more and no less evil than we see around us."

Hacker pondered. There was an uncomfortable wrongness about this child's testimony. She should have been gibbering with fear, when in fact she seemed self-possessed. He wondered if by some strange chance she really had assistance from the devil's minions.

"Charity Payne, thee has confessed to owning second sight. Does thee use this devilish power to spy on thy neighbors?"

It was a telling point. Some among the spectators exchanged discomfited glances.

"Nay, 'tis not devilish, and I cannot see into the doings of my neighbors—except—"

"Speak up, girl. Except what?"

"Once I did perceive by my seeing a most foul murder."

"Murder!" The squire's voice was harsh. A few in the crowd made the sign of the cross.

"Aye. To tell true, two murders. Men whose corpses do now lie buried unshriven in a dark cellar close onto this spot. 'Tween them lies a satchel of golden guineas."

It took a minute for the squire to find his voice.

"A cellar?" he croaked.

"Aye, a root cellar, belike the place one would keep winter apples." She lifted her head and stared straight into the squire's eyes, challenging him to inquire further.

The silence was ponderous as he strove to straighten out his thoughts. To this moment he was safe, for her words described every cellar in and about the village. But she knew. Beyond any question, she knew. Her gaze, seeming to penetrate the darkest corners of his mind, told him that, even more clearly than her words.

Squire Hacker believed in witches and considered them evil and deserving of being destroyed. He had seen and shuddered at the horrible travesty of a lamb in farmer Croft's stable yard, but he had seen like deformities in the Caribbee and did not hold the event an evidence of witchcraft. Not for a minute had he thought Charity a witch, for she showed none of the signs. Her wild talk and the growing rumors had simply seemed to provide the opportunity for some dalliance with a pretty young girl and possibly, in exchange for an acquittal, a lien upon her father's land.

Now he was unsure. She must indeed have second sight to have penetrated his secret, for it had been stormy that night five years ago, and none had seen the missing sailors near to his house. Of that he was confident. Further, shockingly, she knew how and where they lay buried. Another question and answer could not be risked.

He moved his head slowly and looked right and left at the silent throng.

"Charity Payne," he said, picking his words with greatest care, "has put her hand on the Book and sworn to tell true, an act, I opine, she could scarce perform, were she a witch. Does any person differ with me?"

John Hix looked up in startled hopefulness.

"Very well. The lambing at Master Croft's did have the taint of witchcraft, but Master Trowbridge has stated his belief that some noxious plant is growing in Croft's pasture, and 'tis at the least possible. Besides, the ewe is old and she has thrown runty lambs before.

"To quote Master Trowbridge again, he holds that the cholera which has afflicted us so sorely comes from naught but the drinking of bad water. He advises boiling it. I prefer adding a little rum."

He got the laughter he sought. There was a lessening of tension.

"As to second sight." Again he swept the crowd with his gaze. "Charity had laid claim to it, and I called it a devilish

44 •

gift to test her, but second sight is not witchcraft, as ye well know. My own grandmother had it, and a better woman ne'er lived. I hold it to be a gift of God. Would any challenge me?

"Very well. I would warn Charity to be cautious in what she sees and tells, for second sight can lead to grievous disputations. I do not hold with her story of two murdered men although I think that in her own sight she is telling true. If any have aught of knowledge of so dire a crime, I adjure him to step forth and speak."

He waited. "Nobody? Then, by the authority conferred on me by his Excellency the Governor, I declare that Charity Payne is innocent of the charges brought. She may be released."

This was not at all the eventuality which a few of Squire Hacker's cronies had foretold. The crowd had clearly expected a day-long inquisition climaxed by a prisoner to bedevil in the stocks. The squire's aboutface and his abrupt ending of the trial surprised them and angered a few. They stood uncertain.

Then someone shouted hurrah and someone else called for three cheers for Squire Hacker, and all in a minute the gathering had lost its hate and was taking on the look of a picnic. Men headed for the tavern. Parson Hix said a long prayer to which few listened, and everybody gathered around to wring Obie Payne's good hand and to give his daughter a squeeze.

At intervals through the afternoon and evening Peter touched lightly on Charity's mind, finding her carefree and happily occupied with visitors. He chose not to obtrude himself until she called.

Late that night she lay on her mattress and stared into the dark.

"Peter," she whispered.

"Yes, Charity."

"Oh, thank you again."

"Forget it. I got you into the mess. Now you're out of it. Anyway, I didn't really help. It all had to work out the way it did, because that's the way it had happened. You see?"

"No, not truly. How do we know that Squire won't dig up those old bones and burn them?"

"Because he didn't. Four years from now somebody will find them."

"No, Peter, I do not understand, and I am afeared again."

"Why, Charity?"

"It must be wrong, thee and me talking together like this and knowing what is to be and what is not."

"But what could be wrong about it?"

"That I do not know, but I think 'twere better you should stay in your time and me in mine. Goodbye, Peter."

"Charity!"

"And God bless you."

Abruptly she was gone and in Peter's mind there was an emptiness and a knowledge of being alone. He had not known that she could close him out like this.

With the passing of days he became skeptical and in time he might have disbelieved entirely. But Charity visited him again. It was October. He was alone and studying, without much interest.

"Peter."

"Charity, it's you."

"Yes. For a minute, please, Peter, for only a minute, but I had to tell you. I—" She seemed somehow embarrassed. "There is a message."

"A what?"

"Look at Bear Rock, Peter, under the bear's jaw on the left side."

46 •

With that, she was gone.

The cold water swirled around his legs as he traced with one finger the painstakingly chiseled message she had left; a little-girl message in a symbol far older than either of them.

The Seventh Mandarin

Jane Yolen

ONCE IN THE East, where the wind blows gently on the bells of the temple, there lived a king of the highest degree.

He was a good king. And he knew the laws of his land. But of his people he knew nothing at all, for he had never been beyond the high stone walls that surrounded his palace.

All day long the king read about his kingdom in the books and scrolls that were kept in the palace. And all day long he was guarded and guided by the seven mandarins who had lived all their lives, as the king had, within the palace walls.

These mandarins were honorable men. They dressed in silken robes and wore embroidered slippers. They ate from porcelain dishes and drank the most delicate teas.

Now, while it was important that the mandarins guarded and guided their king throughout his days, they had a higher duty still. At night they were the guardians of the king's soul.

It was written in the books and scrolls of the kingdom that each night the king's soul left his body and flew into the sky on the wings of a giant kite. And the king and the seven mandarins believed that what was written in the books and scrolls was true. And so, each mandarin took turns flying the king's kite through the long, dark hours, keeping it high above the terrors of the night.

This kite was a giant dragon. Its tail was of silk with colored tassels. Its body was etched with gold. And when the sun quit that kingdom in the East, the giant kite rose like a serpent in the wind, flown by one of the seven mandarins.

And for uncounted years it was so.

Now, of all the mandarins, the seventh was the youngest. He was also the most simple. While the other mandarins enjoyed feasting and dancing and many rich pleasures, the seventh mandarin loved only three things in all the world. He loved the king, the books and scrolls of the law, and the king's giant kite.

That he loved his king there was no doubt, for the seventh mandarin would not rest until the king rested.

That he loved the books and scrolls there was also no doubt. Not only did the seventh mandarin believe that what was written therein was true. He also believed that what was *not* written was *not* true.

But more than his king and more than the books and scrolls of the law, the seventh mandarin loved the king's kite, the carrier of the king's soul. He could make it dip and soar and crest the currents of air like a falcon trained to his hand.

One night, when it was the turn of the seventh mandarin to fly the king's kite, the sky was black with clouds. A wild wind like no wind before it entered the kingdom.

The seventh mandarin was almost afraid to fly the kite, for he had never seen such a wind. But he knew that he had to send it into the sky. The king's kite *must* fly, or the king's soul would be in danger. And so the seventh mandarin sent the kite aloft.

The minute the giant kite swam into the sky, it began to

rage and strain at the string. It twisted and turned and dived and pulled. The wind gnawed and fretted and goaded the kite, ripping at its tender belly and snatching at its silken tail. At last, with a final snap, the precious kite string parted.

Before the seventh mandarin's eyes, the king's kite sailed wildly over the palace spires, over the roofs of the mandarins' mansions, over the high walls that surrounded the courtyards, and out of sight.

"Come back, come back, O Magnificent Wind Bird," cried the seventh mandarin. "Come back with the king's soul, and I will tip your tail with gold and melt silver onto your wings."

But the kite did not come back.

The seventh mandarin ran down the steps. He put his cape about his face so that no one would know him. He ran through the echoing corridors. He ran past the mandarins' mansions and through the gates of the high palace walls. Then he ran where he had never been before—past the neat houses of the merchants, past the tiny homes of the workers, past the canals that held the peddlers' boats, past the ramshackle, falling-down huts and hovels of the poor.

At last, in the distance, hovering about the hills that marked the edge of the kingdom, the seventh mandarin saw something flutter like a wounded bird in the sky. And though the wind pushed and pulled at his cape and at last tore it from his back, the seventh mandarin did not stop. He ran and ran until he came to the foot of the mountain.

There he found the king's kite. But what a terrible sight met his eyes. The wings of the dragon were dirty and torn. Its tail was shredded and bare. The links of its body were broken apart.

It would never fly again.

The seventh mandarin did not know what to do. He was afraid to return to the palace. It was not that he feared for his own life. He feared for the life of his king. For if the king's soul had flown on the wings of the kite, the king was surely dead.

Yet, much as he was afraid to return, the seventh mandarin was more afraid not to. And so he gathered the king's kite in his arms and began the long, slow journey back.

He carried the king's kite past the canals and the ramshackle, falling-down huts and hovels of the poor. And as he passed with the broken kite in his arms, it came to him that he had never read of such things in the books and scrolls of the kingdom. Yet the cries and groans he heard were not made by the wind.

At last, as the first light of the new day touched the gates of the high palace walls, the seventh mandarin entered the courtyard. He climbed the stairs to his chamber and placed the battered, broken kite on his couch.

Then he sat down and waited to hear of the death of the king.

Scarcely an hour went by before all seven of the mandarins were summoned to the king's chamber. The king lay on his golden bed. His face was pale and still. His hands lay like two withered leaves by his side.

Surely, thought the seventh mandarin, I have killed my king. And he began to weep.

But slowly the king opened his eyes.

"I dreamed a dream last night," he said, his voice low and filled with pain. "I dreamed that in my kingdom there are ramshackle hovels and huts that are falling down."

"It is not so," said the six mandarins, for they had never been beyond the high palace walls and so had never seen such things.

Only the seventh mandarin was silent.

"I dreamed that in my kingdom," continued the king,

"there are people who sigh and moan—people who cry and groan when the night is dark and deep."

"It is not so," said the six mandarins, for they had never read of such things in the books and scrolls.

The seventh mandarin was silent.

"If it is not so," said the king, slowly raising his hand to his head, "then how have I dreamed it? For is it not written that the dream is the eye of the soul? And if my soul was flying on the wings of my kite and these things are not so, then how did my dream see all this?"

The six mandarins were silent.

Then the seventh mandarin spoke. He was afraid, but he spoke. And he said, "O King, I saw these same things last night, and I did not dream!"

The six mandarins looked at the seventh mandarin in astonishment.

But the seventh mandarin continued. "The wind was a wild, mad beast. It ripped your kite from my hands. And the kite flew like an angel in the night to these same huts and hovels of which you dreamed. And there are many who moan and sigh, who groan and cry beyond the high palace walls. There are many—although it is not written in any of the books or scrolls of the kingdom."

Then the seventh mandarin bowed his head and waited for his doom. For it was death to fail the king. And it was death to damage his kite. And it was death to say that what was *not* written in the books and scrolls was so.

Then the king spoke, his voice low and crackling like the pages of an ancient book. "For three reasons that you already know, you deserve to die."

The other mandarins looked at one another and nodded.

"But," said the king, sitting up in his golden bed, "for discovering the truth and not fearing to reveal it, you deserve to live." And he signaled the seventh mandarin to stand at his right hand.

That very night, the king and his seven mandarins made their way to the mountain at the edge of the kingdom. There they buried the king's kite with honors.

And the next morning, when the kingdom awoke, the people found that the high walls surrounding the palace had been leveled to the ground.

As for the king, he never again relied solely upon the laws of the land, but instead rode daily with his mandarins through the kingdom. He met with his people and heard their pleas. He listened and looked as well as read.

The mandarins never again had to fly the king's kite as a duty. Instead, once a year, at a great feast, they sent a giant dragon kite into the sky to remind themselves and their king of the folly of believing only what is written.

And the king, with the seventh mandarin always by his side, ruled a land of good and plenty until he came to the end of his days.

The Voices of El Dorado

Howard Goldsmith

I CAN'T BLAME anyone but myself for the jam I got myself into. Rusty threw down the challenge, but it was my own big mouth that drove him to dare me. And you know how hard it is to back down from a dare, especially when you've been boasting like a puffed-up, loose-tongued bullfrog.

The episode with Rusty took place on a hike one sunny afternoon in early spring. We were returning home from a camping trip through Logan Forest. Our group had never explored that neck of the woods before.

As Rusty unfolded a map of the terrain and checked it against his compass, I remarked that I didn't need any old map to find my way back to Central City. "And only a tenderfoot has to use a compass," I added for good measure.

Rusty's face reddened. It matched the color of his tousled hair. "Well, wise guy, how would *you* get home?" he snapped.

"That's simple enough," I replied offhandedly. "Just by watching the sun and getting directions from its changing position in the sky. And," I added, "by observing what side moss grows on trees."

Rusty threw his head back and gave an imitation of a hog snorting.

I knew what he was thinking. Rusty sometimes led our entire troop on expeditions, and he never let any of us forget it. And he took great pride in the number of merit badges he had earned. I always teased him by saying that Daniel Boone never earned any badges, and he made out pretty well as a scout. And now, finally, I had the chance to show Rusty who was Daniel Boone and who was the tenderfoot.

Rusty leaned forward, the tip of his freckled nose an inch from mine. His chin jutted out challengingly. "If you're so smart, let's see you make it back home all by yourself." His lips curled in a sneering grin.

I smiled inwardly. Rusty was falling right into my trap. I couldn't resist the chance to show him up at scouting, even though I didn't like the idea of traveling home without the other kids.

"Okay," I answered casually, handing him my compass. "Please take care of this for me. Some people are born campers, and others just don't have what it takes. I'll be glad to give you a demonstration of practical know-how."

Rusty stood there fuming as I slung my pack over my back, gave a careless wave, and set off jauntily into the forest.

I glanced back over my shoulder. Our leader hadn't noticed my abrupt departure. Rusty's face had broken out into red blotches. One of his feet beat an angry tattoo on the ground. The other kids were laughing and enjoying his discomfort.

What I had concealed from Rusty was the fact that my father had taken me on an overnight hike through Logan Forest the previous summer. We had camped near the very spot where the group was now staying. Dad had pointed out that Clear Creek, which was located close by, narrowed to a stream that led straight to Central City. It would be a cinch to find Clear Creek, and from there it would be smooth sailing.

There was no trail to guide me, but I was pretty sure of my bearings. I remembered the clump of oak trees my father and I had passed through. I plunged deeper and deeper into the forest.

Sunlight painted the woods a blaze of gold and green. Feathery branches cast lacy shadows along the ground. On leafy boughs, birds twittered and jerked their heads in my direction, and grasshoppers darted and disappeared in the shadows.

After groping around in the brush for half an hour, my confidence began to wilt. I knew how to make it home from the creek. The only problem was that the creek seemed to have disappeared.

I had been heading east. I veered about sharply and struck off in a westerly direction. But after trudging for an hour, I began to wonder if I'd ever make it home. Suddenly I heard the sound of water rippling in the distance. I raced through a thicket in the direction of the gurgling sounds and emerged at the edge of a stream.

"You see," I said to myself, with a deep sigh of relief, "there was nothing to worry about. You just temporarily lost your sense of direction. It could happen to anyone. Now, if I follow the stream north, I'll reach home within an hour. And will I gloat the next time I see Rusty!"

I walked steadily for an hour. I just had to be approaching Central City. But there were no signs of civilization. Instead, the forest became denser and darker. I began a slow jog.

It wasn't long before I was out of breath. I stumbled along, panting and staggering under the weight of my pack. My face was grimy and prickly with sweat. My legs ached and my feet burned. I would certainly remember this hike for a long time to come!

My watch indicated that I'd been following the stream for two hours, and Central City was still nowhere in sight. Suddenly it dawned on me that I must have been following an entirely different stream, one that had been leading me farther into the depths of the forest.

I stopped abruptly. I tried to keep cool and consider my position. I forced my mind to work against the mounting numbness that invaded it. I could double back along the path of the stream. But even if I managed to locate my starting point, which way would I then turn?

I decided to continue tracking the unfamiliar stream. It must lead *somewhere*. Perhaps to another town. Turning back might only land me in a deeper muddle.

The sun was beginning to set. The sky glowed with streaks of florid color. The dying glow of sunset lent a pale, mysterious cast to the forest. Arching trees engulfed me in their dark, leafy foliage.

Then, through a break in the woods, I spied a dark jumble of buildings off in the distance. A town! At last!

When I finally reached the clearing, I could see that the town was situated about a hundred yards west of a range of hills that enclosed a deep canyon. I ran toward the town with all the strength that remained in my wobbly legs.

As I approached the nearest houses, I stopped short. The buildings stretched out before me now—if you could call those ramshackle boxes "buildings." The town was completely deserted! With a heavy, sinking feeling, I read the name of the town on an old weathered sign that swung from a rusty nail: EL DORADO.

I stamped my foot in disgust. It was just my luck to have discovered a ghost town! I marched wearily down its gloomy street, kicking up clouds of dust.

El Dorado must have been one of the many mining towns that had sprung up during the Gold Rush of the 1850s. Prospectors, seeking the precious metal, had trooped through the hills of Colorado by the thousands. The town had probably been abandoned more than a hundred years ago.

Well, a ghost town was better than no town at all—providing there were no real ghosts in it! Anyway, it was only a matter of spending the night.

I walked up and down the street, examining the old frame buildings. Most of them looked ready to collapse with the slightest shove. I picked out the one that seemed the sturdiest. At least there weren't any big holes in the roof.

Weeds grew up to the threshold and pressed against the door. I turned the doorknob. The door scraped open with a rusty scream of its hinges. A spider skittered out of my way and scurried up the opposite wall. The dusky interior had the dank, musty odor of rotted wood. One side of the shack had a blank rectangle for a window. Long, shadowy fingers stretched across the floor.

Up to that moment, I had forgotten how long it was since I had last eaten. I dumped my knapsack on the floor, took out a sandwich, and made quick work of it. Then I unfolded my bedroll and lay down to sleep.

Through the empty window, icy moonbeams fell upon my face. Outside it was deathly still. I felt the presence of the vast, gaping canyon nearby. It was like being alone on the edge of the earth.

I tried not to let my imagination run away with me, or I'd soon be seeing strange shapes and hearing unearthly sounds. I had enough real, practical problems without inventing imaginary ones.

I was getting a grip on myself when a howling wind suddenly rustled up from the canyon. It played with the shack like an angry child with a dollhouse, rattling it to and fro. I buried my head deep into my bedroll. The boards of the shack groaned and creaked around me.

All at once, my ears caught a strange sound. Sitting up straight, I strained to hear.

Miaow . . . miaow!

A *cat*? Out here in a ghost town? Couldn't be! A mountain lion maybe!

Terror seized me. Cold shivers ran up my spine. With trembling fingers, I drew my Boy Scout knife from its sheath. Staring at the open window, I waited for whatever it was to spring through.

The cry came again, more distinctly this time. I cocked my ear.

It wasn't *miaow*, but a girl's voice!

"MOTHER! MOTHER!"

Another voice followed—the unmistakable cry of a boy. "FATHER! FATHER!"

What was going on? Who could they be? What were they doing out here in this desolate place?

"Who is it?" I called.

No answer.

"Who is it?" I shouted louder.

Still no answer.

I fumbled around in my knapsack for a flashlight. Gripping it tightly, I scrambled out of the bedroll, sprang to my feet, and swung the door open.

I flashed a beam along the dark, dusty street.

"Who's out there?" I yelled.

No reply.

My flashlight probed every corner and crevice of the street. No one was there.

I turned around and crept back into the shack. No sooner

had I lain down than the voices began again, urgently and insistently.

"MOTHER! MOTHER!"

"FATHER! FATHER!"

On and on the voices wailed.

"SAVE US! SAVE US!"

"COME BACK! COME BACK!"

I leaped up and rushed to the door. But the moment I opened it, the voices ceased.

"Who's calling?" I shouted hoarsely. "Why won't you answer me?"

No reply.

I didn't know what to think. Puzzled and frightened, I went back in again. How could I help them if they wouldn't answer? They seemed to be playing a cat-and-mouse game with me.

I lay down, resolved not to pay attention if the voices returned.

The wind picked up, whipping billows of dust through the open window. The voices came floating back on the midnight air. The strange, pitiful cries were louder than ever before.

"MOTHER! MOTHER!"

"SAVE US! SAVE US!"

I buried myself in my bedroll and lay there quivering. I pressed my hands over my ears, but the eerie voices droned on and on.

I sat up, grabbed a roll of gauze from my pack, ripped off two pieces, and stuffed them in my ears. But the voices would not be muffled. One barely stopped when the other began. Minutes ticked by endlessly as I tossed and turned, unable to sleep.

Finally, toward dawn, I dozed off. But my dreams were troubled, and when I awoke, I felt almost as tired as the night before. My bones ached. I stood up, stretched, and yawned.

The empty window made a brilliant rectangle of light on the floor.

I opened the door, inhaled the dry, thin mountain air, and shook the cobwebs out of my head. I felt better in the clear light of morning.

My legs itched to get moving, but I had no idea how to find my way home from this place. If I set out into the woods, I might end up walking in circles and, by nightfall, find myself in an even worse predicament. And there was no telling when there might be a sharp drop in temperature. But here, at least, was shelter. I had enough food in my pack to last me for a few days, if necessary, and there was a stream nearby for water. I really shouldn't worry so much—a rescue party was surely combing the woods for me at that very moment.

But though I brightened a bit at this thought, I still felt completely, desolately alone. And the possibility of spending another night in that shack filled me with dread. I couldn't figure out where the voices had come from. Why had the boy and girl ignored my calls?

I decided to look for them. I poked around inside the empty shacks. The floors were caked with dust and wind-blown sand. There was no sign that anyone had entered them in years.

My thoughts returned to the rescue party. Perhaps they would send a helicopter to scour the terrain. I raced into the woods, gathered up some kindling, and stacked it in a small pile on the edge of town. I ran back into the shack and took a box of matches out of my pack. After stuffing the matches into my pocket, I felt better. The moment I heard the distant whine of a motor, I would dash to the woodpile and set it aflame.

But what if the kindling failed to ignite? Then I'd wave my arms like a windmill. I practiced revolving my arms until they ached. I thought I'd better save them for the crucial moment.

Now that I'd reviewed my situation, I began to feel a bit more cheerful. I'd surely be rescued before evening. With a light spring to my step, I set out for a stroll around the rim of the canyon.

The vast cavity yawned up at me. Sharp-ridged hills rose to towering heights around me. I edged closer to the rim for a better look. "Careful," I told myself, "that's a drop of three hundred feet, at least."

Taking a step back, I began to test the canyon for echoes. I shouted my name, "Tim, Tim."

As my voice rebounded, I was shocked to hear another voice follow it. "HUSH, HUSH."

And then another. "BE STILL, STILL."

"Who is it?" I cried. "IT? IT?" my voice echoed.

There was no answer.

"I heard you," I called again. "YOU, YOU," pealed my voice in slowly dying eddies.

"I know you're there. THERE, THERE."

Still no answer.

I thought of a trick. I turned around and started back to the shack. But after walking thirty yards, I ducked swiftly behind a bush and waited.

After a few minutes, I heard the echo of a girl's voice reverberating through the canyon. "HE'LL NEVER FIND US, FIND US."

"NEVER, NEVER," a boy responded.

"HE HAS NO RIGHT HERE, HERE," echoed the girl's voice.

"THE MOUNTAINS BELONG TO US, US," replied the boy.

I sprang out of hiding and dashed to the rim of the canyon. "Who are you? YOU, YOU?"

"SHHH! THE BOY! BOY!"

"HE'S BACK! BACK!"

A volley of echoes bounced along the walls of the canyon.

"HA, HA, HA."

"HE THINKS HE'LL FIND US, FIND US."

I whirled about with dizzy speed. The voices were in back of me, now in front, now in back again. They were taunting me. The boy and girl must have been able to see me, but however hard I tried, I couldn't see them. "I must find them," I told myself.

"HE'LL NEVER FIND US, FIND US," came a voice, as if reading my mind.

But now I thought I was on to them. Their voices seemed to come from one of the hollows dug into the side of the canyon. I leaned over the edge to get a better view and then stepped gingerly onto an over-hanging shelf. I was just easing my second foot down when the shelf suddenly gave way and crumbled beneath my feet! With a shock of terror, I found myself slipping down the slope. Frantically, I searched for a foothold, but there was not a fissure or cleft to support me. My hands clutched and clawed at the hill as it raced by my groping fingers. I plunged screaming down the hill until, suddenly, I landed with an abrupt thud.

Shaken and bruised, I couldn't help but be relieved. At least I hadn't landed in the deep rocky pit of the canyon. But when I looked around, creeping fear rippled along my arms, legs, my whole body. I found myself on a slightly projecting ledge, with only about four feet of rocky floor beneath me!

Clinging desperately to the side of the hill, not knowing what to do next, I looked up, hopelessly searching the crest of the hill. I didn't know what I was looking for. There was no way I could get back to the top. My breath came in heaving gasps. My head was spinning. I strained my neck farther upward. I had to keep my eyes away from what loomed below me. Then, slowly, something took shape before my eyes. I blinked again and again, trying to get the dust out. Then I realized I had been staring at a dwarf birch tree that jutted out at an angle from a ridge near the top of the rise. Could I possibly reach it? I really didn't know. It rose almost seven feet above the far end of the ledge I stood on. If I could only grab it, I might be able to pull myself up to safety. It was perilous but not impossible. I was good at high jumping. I had to take the risk. There was no telling how long I could remain erect on that narrow ledge.

Cautiously I sidled along the ledge, hugging the slope of the hill. "Slowly, slowly," I told myself. "There's no hurry. Easy does it."

Dripping perspiration, I finally reached the spot. I stared up at the tree. My heart pounded wildly. I gritted my teeth and said a silent prayer. Then, straining upward as high as my arms could reach, I vaulted up at the tree. Slap! My hands made contact. I locked my fingers firmly around the trunk. Using every ounce of strength, I drew myself up, inch by painful inch.

All at once the tree began to bend and sway. I bobbed up and down like a puppet. Praying that the scrawny birch was strong enough to support me, I continued pulling myself up until I succeeded in wrapping both my arms around it. But suddenly the tree gave a wrench and pitched sharply downward. It was tearing loose from its roots!

I hung suspended over the canyon, my eyes shut tight. I dared not breathe. The tree was shaking violently. And as my heart drummed and my head whirled, those same mysterious voices swelled throughout the canyon.

"HE'S FALLING! FALLING!" The echoes had lost their taunt, suddenly.

"HELP HIM! HELP HIM!" came the girl's voice. It was, unexpectedly, almost gentle.

"WE MUST, MUST, MUST."

The tree snapped erect, as if held by invisible bands. Without a moment's hesitation, I pulled myself up. My arms encircled the trunk. The tree was still holding firm. I could hardly believe it. With one last supreme effort, I heaved myself up and over the cliff. Then, as if suddenly released from the grip of an unseen power, the tree tore loose and plunged down the hill.

I stretched out on the ground, panting and sobbing with relief. In my mind there was no doubt that some friendly force had kept the tree from falling until I had climbed to safety. A picture of two children, a boy and a girl, flashed before my eyes. I could imagine them straightening the tree as I hung suspended over the canyon. I owed my life to them.

"Thank you! Thank you!" I cried fervently. My voice reverberated as I stumbled to my feet.

I waited expectantly, but no answer came. Still I waited, standing there for minutes, hoping. But not a sound disturbed the pervading stillness of the yawning canyon.

Finally, I lowered my head dejectedly and turned to leave. As I did, voices rang out behind me.

"WE ARE ONLY ECHOES, ECHOES, ECHOES."

I spun about sharply. "You have no bodies? BODIES?"

A girl's voice cried, "WE ARE ONLY ECHOES, ECHOES, ECHOES."

And then came a boy's voice. "WAITING, WAITING, WAITING."

And then silence.

There was no use. They didn't want me to know who they were. I trudged on back to the shack.

Pacing back and forth in the shack, wondering what to do next, I suddenly heard footsteps.

"Tim! Tim!" a man's voice called. It was my father's voice!

I raced out the door. There was my father striding down the street at the head of a rescue party. His face was drawn and anxious. I ran into his arms. He examined me to see if I was all right.

"Tim," he said, "we were worried sick about you. We've been out searching all night. Then Mr. Bailey remembered this old ghost town and figured you might have come here. It was a good guess."

He turned to Mr. Bailey and thanked him. Mr. Bailey's leathery, weather-beaten face creased into a big grin.

Breathlessly I blurted out my experience with the echoes. Everyone gave me a strange look. They thought I was out of my mind with fatigue and fright. All except Mr. Bailey, who leaned forward with a look of keen interest.

"Hmm," he said, stroking his chin thoughtfully. "You know, I recall an old legend that used to circulate around mining camps. This is reaching far back in my memory. These hills are pitted with scores of caves and recesses, you know. The story has it that two children once wandered into a cave in this very canyon. Rescue parties searched for days, but all their efforts amounted to nothing. From time to time, they caught the distant sound of voices echoing on the wind. But the faint cries never lasted long enough to be located. The poor tykes must have weakened pretty quickly without food or water. The story has it that their restless spirits haunt the canyon, their plaintive cries forever echoing through the hills. According to the Legend of the Lost Children, they linger as echoes to keep vigil until their parents return to find them."

Mr. Bailey held us spellbound with his tale.

"Oh, who believes those old miners' tales," scoffed a gravel-voiced, barrel-chested man with dark stubble covering his face. "They're just campfire stories invented to pass the time. Nobody puts any stock in 'em."

Everyone nodded in agreement except Mr. Bailey. He scratched his face and drawled, "I wouldn't be so sure."

As we prepared to leave, we suddenly heard my name called. "TIM, TIM."

Everyone gave a start. "What was that?" they asked with one voice.

Then they all stared at me. They knew, suddenly, that Mr. Bailey's story was true.

I whispered good-bye to the children, relieved that they had been there to save me from death but more than a little sad that they had not ever had anyone to help them.

And as we drove off, the dust kicking behind us, I thought that I heard the sound of weeping.

The Box

Bruce Coville

ONCE THERE WAS a boy who had a box.

The boy's name was Michael, and the box was very special because it had been given to him by an angel.

Michael knew it had been an angel because of the huge white wings he wore. So he took very good care of the box, because the angel had asked him to.

And he never, ever opened it.

When Michael's mother asked him where he had gotten the box, he said, "An angel gave it to me."

"That's nice, dear," she answered, and went back to stirring her cake mix.

Michael carried the box with him wherever he went. He took it to school. He took it out to play. He set it by his place at mealtimes.

After all, he never knew when the angel would come back and ask for it.

The box was very beautiful. It was made of dark wood and carved with strange designs. The carvings were smooth and polished, and they seemed to glow whenever they caught the light. A pair of tiny golden hinges, and a miniature

golden latch that Michael never touched, held the cover tight to the body of the box.

Michael loved the way it felt against his fingers.

Sometimes Michael's friends would tease him about the box.

"Hey, Michael," they would say. "How come you never come out to play without that box?"

"Because I am taking care of it for an angel," he would answer. And because this was true, the boys would leave him alone.

At night, before he went to bed, he would rub the box with a soft cloth to make it smooth and glossy.

Sometimes when he did this he could hear something moving inside the box.

He wondered how it was that something could stay alive in the box without any food or water.

But he did not open the box. The angel had asked him not to.

One night when he was lying in his bed, Michael heard a voice.

"Give me the box," it said.

Michael sat up.

"Who are you?" he asked.

"I am the angel," said the voice. "I have come for my box."

"You are not my angel," shouted Michael. He was beginning to grow frightened.

"Your angel has sent me. Give me the box."

"No. I can only give it to my angel."

"Give me the box!"

"No!" cried Michael.

There was a roar, and a rumble of thunder. A cold wind came shrieking through his bedroom.

"I must have that box!" sobbed the voice, as though its heart was breaking.

"No! No!" cried Michael, and he clutched the box tightly to his chest.

But the voice was gone.

Soon Michael's mother came in to comfort him, telling him he must have had a bad dream. After a time he stopped crying and went back to sleep.

But he knew the voice had been no dream.

After that night Michael was twice as careful with the box as he had been before. He grew to love it deeply. It reminded him of his angel.

As Michael grew older the box became more of a problem for him.

His teachers began to object to him keeping it constantly at his side or on his desk. One particularly thick and unbending teacher even sent him to the principal. But when Michael told the principal he was taking care of the box for an angel, the principal told Mrs. Jenkins to leave him alone.

When Michael entered junior high he found that the other boys no longer believed him when he told them why he carried the box. He understood that. They had never seen the angel, as he had. Most of the children were so used to the box by now that they ignored it anyway.

But some of the boys began to tease Michael about it.

One day two boys grabbed the box and began a game of keep-away with it, throwing it back and forth above Michael's head, until one of them dropped it.

It landed with an ugly smack against the concrete.

Michael raced to the box and picked it up. One of the fine corners was smashed flat, and a piece of one of the carvings had broken off.

"I hate you," he started to scream. But the words choked in his throat, and the hate died within him.

He picked up the box and carried it home. Then he cried for a little while.

The boys were very sorry for what they had done. But they never spoke to Michael after that, and secretly they hated him, because they had done something so mean to him, and he had not gotten mad.

For seven nights after the box was dropped Michael did not hear any noise inside it when he was cleaning it.

He was terrified.

What if everything was ruined? What could he tell the angel? He couldn't eat or sleep. He refused to go to school. He simply sat beside the box, loving it and caring for it.

On the eighth day he could hear the movements begin once more, louder and stronger than ever.

He sighed, and slept for eighteen hours.

When he entered high school Michael did not go out for sports, because he was not willing to leave the box alone. He certainly could not take it out onto a football field with him.

He began taking art classes instead. He wanted to learn to paint the face of his angel. He tried over and over again, but he could never get the pictures to come out the way he wanted them to.

Everyone else thought they were beautiful.

But they never satisfied Michael.

Whenever Michael went out with a girl she would ask him what he had in the box. When he told her he didn't know, she would not believe him. So then he would tell her the story of how the angel had given him the box. Then the girl would think he was fooling her. Sometimes a girl would try to open the box when he wasn't looking.

But Michael always knew, and whenever a girl did this, he would never ask her out again.

Finally Michael found a girl who believed him. When he told her that an angel had given him the box, and that he had to take care of it for him, she nodded her head as if this was the most sensible thing she had ever heard.

Michael showed her the pictures he had painted of his angel.

They fell in love, and after a time they were married.

Things were not so hard for Michael now, because he had someone who loved him to share his problems with.

But it was still not easy to care for the box. When he tried to get a job people would ask him why he carried it, and usually they would laugh at him. More than once he was fired from his work because his boss would get sick of seeing the box and not being able to find out what was in it.

Finally Michael found work as a night custodian. He carried the box in a little knapsack on his back, and did his job so well that no one ever questioned him.

One night Michael was driving to work. It was raining, and very slippery. A car turned in front of him. There was an accident, and both Michael and the box flew out of the car.

When Michael woke up he was in the hospital. The first thing he asked for was his box. But it was not there.

Michael jumped out of bed, and it took three nurses and two doctors to wrestle him back into it. They gave him a shot to make him sleep.

That night, when the hospital was quiet, Michael snuck out of bed and got his clothes.

It was a long way to where he had had the accident, and he had to walk the whole distance. He searched for hours under the light of a bright, full moon, until finally he found the box. It was caked with mud, and another of the beautiful corners had been flattened in. But none of the carvings were broken, and when he held it to his ear, he could hear something moving inside.

When the nurse came in to check him in the morning, she found Michael sleeping peacefully, with a dirty box beside him on the bed. When she reached out to take it, his hand wrapped around the box and held it in a grip of steel. He did not even wake up.

Michael would have had a hard time paying the hospital bills. But one day a man came to their house and saw some of his paintings. He asked if he could buy one. Other people heard about them, and before long Michael was selling many paintings. He quit his night job, and began to make his living as an artist.

But he was never able to paint a picture of the angel that looked the way it should.

One night when Michael was almost thirty he heard the voice again.

"Give me the box!" it cried, in tones so strong and stern that Michael was afraid he would obey them.

But he closed his eyes, and in his mind he saw his angel again, with his face so strong and his eyes so full of love, and he paid no attention to the voice at all.

The next morning Michael went to his easel and began to paint. It was the most beautiful picture he had ever made.

But still it did not satisfy him.

The voice came after Michael seven times that year, but he was never tempted to answer it again.

Michael and his wife had two children, and they loved them very much. The children were always curious about the box their father carried, and one day, when Michael was napping, the oldest child tried to open it.

Michael woke and saw what was happening. For the first time in his memory he lost his temper.

He raised his hand to strike his son.

But in the face of his child he suddenly saw the face of the angel he had met only once, so long ago, and the anger died within him.

After that day the children left the box alone.

Time went on. The children grew up and went to their own homes. Michael and his wife grew old. The box suffered another accident or two. It was battered now, and even the careful polishing Michael gave it every night did not hide the fact that the carvings were growing thin from the pressure of his hands against them so many hours a day.

Once, when they were very old, Michael's wife said to him, "Do you really think the angel will come back for his box?"

"Hush, my darling," said Michael, putting his finger against her lips.

And she never knew if Michael believed the angel would come back or not.

After a time she grew sick, and died, and Michael was left alone.

Everybody in his town knew who he was, and when he could not hear they called him "Crazy Michael," and whirled their fingers around their ears, and whispered that he had carried that box from the time he was eight years old.

Of course nobody really believed such a silly story.

But they all knew Michael was crazy.

Even so, in their hearts they wished they had a secret as enduring as the one that Crazy Michael carried.

One night, when Michael was almost ninety years old, the angel returned to him and asked for the box.

"Is it really you?" cried Michael. He struggled to his elbows to squint at the face above him. Then he could see that it was indeed the angel, who had not changed a bit in eighty years, while he had grown so old.

"At last," he said softly. "Where have you been all this time, Angel?"

"I have been working," said the angel. "And waiting." He knelt by Michael's bed. "Have you been faithful?"

"I have," whispered Michael.

"Give me the box, please."

Under the pillow, beside his head, the battered box lay waiting. Michael pulled it out and extended it to the angel.

"It is not as beautiful as when you first gave it to me," he said, lowering his head.

"That does not matter," said the angel.

He took the box from Michael's hands. Holding it carefully, he stared at it, as if he could see what was inside. Then he smiled.

"It is almost ready."

Michael smiled too. "What is it?" he asked. His face seemed to glow with happiness. "Tell me what it is at last."

"I cannot," whispered the angel sadly.

Michael's smile crumpled. "Then tell me this," he said after a moment. "Is it important?" His voice was desperate.

"It will change the world," replied the angel.

Michael leaned back against his pillow. "Then surely I will know what it is when this has come to pass," he said, smiling once again.

"No. You will not know," answered the angel.

"But if it is so important that it will change the world, then . . ."

"*You* have changed the world, Michael. How many people know that?"

The angel shimmered and began to disappear.

Michael stretched out his hand. "Wait!" he cried.

The angel reached down. He took Michael's withered hand and held it tightly in his own.

"You have done well," he whispered.

He kissed Michael softly on the forehead.

And then he was gone.

The Lake

Ray Bradbury

THEY CUT THE sky down to my size and threw it over the Michigan lake, put some kids yelling on yellow sand with bouncing balls, a gull or two, a criticizing parent, and me breaking out of a wet wave and finding this world bleary and moist.

I ran up on the beach.

Mama swabbed me with a furry towel. "Stand there and dry," she said.

I stood there and watched the sun take away the water beads on my arms. I replaced them with goose pimples.

"My, there's a wind," said Mama. "Put on your sweater."

"Wait'll I watch my goose bumps," I said.

"Harold," said Mama.

I inserted me into my sweater and watched the waves come up and fall down on the beach. But not clumsily. On purpose, with a green sort of elegance. Even a drunken man could not collapse with such elegance as those waves.

It was September. In the last days when things are getting sad for no reason. The beach was so long and lonely with only about six people on it. The kids quit bouncing the ball because somehow the wind made them sad, too, whistling the way it did, and they sat down and felt autumn come along the long beach.

All the hot dog places were boarded up with strips of golden planking, sealing in all the mustard, onion, meat odors of the long, joyful summer. It was like nailing summer into a series of coffins. One by one the places slammed their covers down, padlocked their doors, and the wind came and touched the sand, blowing away all of the million footprints of July and August. It got so that now, in September, there was nothing but the mark of my rubber tennis shoes and Donald and Delaus Schabold's feet, and their father down by the water curve.

Sand blew up in curtains on the sidewalks, and the merry-go-round was hidden with canvas, all the horses frozen in midair on their brass poles, showing teeth, galloping on. With only the wind for music, slipping through canvas.

I stood there. Everyone else was in school. I was not. Tomorrow I would be on my way westward across the United States on a train. Mom and I had come to the beach for one last brief moment.

There was something about the loneliness that made me want to get away by myself. "Mama, I want to run up the beach aways," I said.

"All right, but hurry back, and don't go near the water."

I ran. Sand spun under me and the wind lifted me. You know how it is, running, arms out so you feel veils from your fingers, caused by wind. Like wings.

Mama withdrew into the distance, sitting. Soon she was only a brown speck and I was all alone. Being alone is a newness to a twelve-year-old child. He is so used to having people around. The only way he can be alone is in his mind. That's why children imagine such fantastic things. There are so many real people around, telling children what and how to do, that a boy has to run off down a beach, even if it's only in his mind, to get by himself in his own world with his own miniature values.

So now I was really alone.

I went down to the water and let it cool up to my stomach. Always before, with the crowd, I hadn't dared to look. But now— Sawing a man in half. A magician. Water is like that. It feels as if you were sawed in half and part of you, sugar, is dissolving away. Cool water, and once in a while a very elegantly stumbling wave that fell with a flourish of lace.

I called her name. A dozen times I called it.

"Tally! Tally! Oh, Tally!"

Funny, but you really expect answers to your calling when you are young. You feel that whatever you may think can be real. And sometimes maybe that is not so wrong.

I thought of Tally, swimming out into the water last May, with her pigtails trailing, blond. She went laughing, and the sun was on her small twelve-year-old shoulders. I thought of the water settling quiet, of the lifeguard leaping into it, of Tally's mother screaming, and how Tally never came out . . .

The lifeguard tried to persuade her to come out, but she did not. He came back with only bits of water weed in his big knuckled fingers, and Tally was gone. She would not sit across from me at school any longer, or chase indoor balls on the brick street on summer nights. She had gone too far out, and the lake would not let her come back in.

And now in the lonely autumn when the sky was huge and the water was huge and the beach was so very long, I had come down for the last time, alone.

I called her name over and over. "Tally, oh, Tally!"

The wind blew so very softly, over my ears, the way wind blows over the mouths of seashells and sets them whispering. The water rose and embraced my chest and then to my knees, and up and down, one way and another, sucking under my heels.

"Tally! Come back, oh, Tally!"

I was only twelve. But I know how much I loved her. It was that love that comes before all significance of body and morals. It was that love that is no more bad than wind and sea and sand lying side by side forever. It was made of all the warm long days together at the beach, and the humming quiet days of droning education at the school. All the long autumn days of the years past when I had carried her books home from school.

"Tally!"

I called her name for the last time. I shivered. I felt water on my face and did not know how it got there. The waves had not splashed that high.

Turning, I retreated to the sand and stood there for half an hour, hoping for one glimpse, one sign, one little bit of Tally to remember. Then, in a sort of symbol, I knelt and built a castle of sand, shaping it fine and building it up as Tally and I had often built them, so many of them. But this time I only built half of it. Then I got up.

"Tally, if you hear me, come in and build the rest."

I began to walk off toward that faraway speck that was Mama. The water came in and blended the sea castle circle by circle, smashing it down little by little, into the original smoothness.

I could not help but think that there are no castles in life that one builds that some wave does not spread down into the old, old formlessness.

Silently, I walked up the beach.

Far away, a merry-go-round jangled faintly, but it was only the wind.

I went away on the train the next day.

Across the cornlands of Illinois. A train has a poor mem-

ory. It soon puts all behind it. It forgets the rivers of childhood, the bridges, the lakes, the valleys, the cottages, the
pains and joys. It spreads them out behind and they drop
back of a horizon.

I lengthened my bones, put flesh on them, changed my
young mind for an older one, threw away clothes as they no
longer fitted, shifted from grammar to high school, to college books, to law books. And then there was a young
woman in Sacramento, there was a preacher, and there were
words and kisses.

I continued with my law study. By the time I was twenty-
two, I had almost forgotten what the East was like.

Margaret suggested that our delayed honeymoon trip be
taken back in that direction.

A train works both ways, like a memory. It brings rushing
back all those things you left behind so many years before.

Lake Bluff, population ten thousand, came up over the
sky. Margaret looked so handsome in her fine new clothes.
She kept watching me as I watched my old world gather me
back into its living. Her strong white hands held onto mine
as the train slid into Bluff Station and our baggage was
escorted out.

So many years, and the things they do to people's faces
and bodies. When we walked through the town, arm in arm,
I saw no one I recognized. There were faces with echoes in
them. Echoes of hikes on ravine trails. Faces with small
laughter in them from closed grammar schools and swinging on metal-linked swings and going up and down on tee-
ter-totters. But I didn't speak. I just walked and looked and
filled up inside with all those memories, like leaves stacked
for burning in autumn.

Our days were happy there. Two weeks in all, revisiting all
the places together. I thought I loved Margaret very well. At
least I thought I did.

It was on one of the last days that we walked down by the shore. It was not quite as late in the year as that day so many years before, but the first evidences of desertion were coming upon the beach. The people were thinning out, several of the hot dog places had been shuttered and nailed, and the wind, as always, had been waiting there to sing for us.

I almost saw Mama sitting on the sand as she used to sit. I had that feeling again of wanting to be alone. But I could not force myself to say it to Margaret. I only held onto her and waited.

It got late in the day. Most of the children had gone home, and only a few men and women remained basking in the windy sun.

The lifeguard boat pulled up on the shore. The lifeguard stepped out of it, slowly, with something in his arms.

I froze there. I held my breath and I felt small, only twelve years old, very little, very infinitesimal and afraid. The wind howled. I could not see Margaret. I could see only the beach, the lifeguard slowly emerging from his boat with a gray sack in his hands, not very heavy, and his face almost as gray and lined.

"Stay here, Margaret," I said. I don't know why I said it.

"But why?"

"Just stay here, that's all—"

I walked slowly down the sand to where the lifeguard stood. He looked at me.

"What is it?" I asked.

The lifeguard kept looking at me for a long time and he couldn't speak. He put the gray sack down on the sand, the water whispered wet around it and went back.

"What is it?" I insisted.

"She's dead," said the lifeguard quietly.

I waited.

• 91

"Funny," he said softly, "funniest thing I ever saw. She's been dead—a long time."

I repeated his words. "A long time?"

"Ten years, I'd say. There haven't been any children drowned here *this* year. There were twelve children drowned here since 1933, but we recovered all their bodies before a few hours had passed. All except one, I remember. This body here, why it must be ten years in the water. It's not—pleasant."

"Open it," I said. I don't know why I said it. The wind was louder.

He fumbled with the sack. "The way I know it's a little girl is because she's still wearing a locket. There's nothing much else to tell by—"

"Hurry, man, *open it!*" I cried.

"I better not do that," he said. Then maybe he saw the way my face must have looked. "She was such a little girl—"

He opened it only partway. That was enough.

The beach was deserted. There was only the sky and the wind and the water and the autumn coming on lonely. I looked down at her there.

I said something, over and over. The lifeguard looked at me. "Where did you find her?" I asked.

"Down the beach, in the shallow water. Down that way. It's a long, long time for her, ain't it?"

I shook my head.

"Yes, it is. Oh God, yes it is."

I thought, people grow. I have grown. But she has not changed. She is still small. She is still young. Death does not permit growth or change. She still has golden hair. She will be forever young and I will love her forever, oh God, I will love her forever.

The lifeguard tied up the sack again.

Down the beach, a few moments later, I walked by myself.

I found something I didn't really expect. This is where the lifeguard found her body, I said to myself.

There, at the water's edge, lay a sand castle, only half built. Just like Tally and I used to make them. She—half. And I—half.

I looked at it. This is where they found Tally. I knelt beside the sand castle and saw the little prints of feet coming in from the lake and going back out to the lake again—and not returning ever.

Then—I knew.

"I'll help you to finish it," I said.

I did. I built the rest of it up very slowly, and then I arose and turned away and walked off, so as not to watch it crumble in the waves, as all things crumble.

I walked back up the beach to where a strange woman named Margaret waited for me, smiling. . . .

A Dozen of Everything

··

Marion Zimmer Bradley

WHEN MARCIE unwrapped the cut-glass bottle, she thought it was perfume. "Oh fine," she said to herself sardonically, "Here I am, being married in four days, and without a rag to wear, and Aunt Hepsibah sends me perfume!"

It wasn't that Marcie was mercenary. But Aunt Hepsibah was, as the vulgar expression puts it, rolling in dough; and she spent about forty dollars a year. She lived in Egypt, in a little mud hut, because, as she said, she wanted to Soak Up the Flavor of the East . . . in large capitals. She wrote Marcie, who was her only living relative, long incoherent letters about the Beauty of the Orient, and the Delights of Contemplation; letters which Marcie dutifully read and as dutifully answered with "Dear Aunt Hepsibah; I hope you are well . . ."

She sighed, and examined the label. Printed in a careful, vague Arabic script, it read "Djinn Number Seven." Marcie shrugged.

Oh well, she thought, it's probably very chi-chi and expensive. If I go without lunch this week, I can manage to get myself a fancy negligee, and maybe a pair of new gloves to wear to the church. Greg will like the perfume, and if I keep my job for a few months after we're married, we'll get along. Of course, Emily Post says that a bride should have a dozen of everything, but we can't *all* be lucky.

She started to put the perfume into her desk drawer—for her lunch hour was almost over—then, on an impulse, she began carefully to work the stopper loose. "I'll just take a tiny sniff—" she thought . . .

The stopper stuck; Marcie twitched, pulled—choked at the curious, pervasive fragrance which stole out. "It sure is strong—" she thought, holding the loosened stopper in her hand . . . then she blinked and dropped it to the floor, where the precious cut glass shattered into a million pieces.

Marcie was a normal child of her generation, which is to say, she went to the movies regularly. She had seen *Sinbad the Sailor,* and *The Thief of Bagdad,* so, of course, she knew immediately what was happening, as the pervasive fragrance rolled out and coalesced into a huge, towering figure with a vaguely oriental face. "My gosh . . ." she breathed, then, as she noticed imminent peril to the office ceiling, directed "Hey, stick your head out the window—quick!"

"To hear is to obey," said the huge figure sibilantly, "but, O mistress, if I might venture to make a suggestion, that might attract attention. Permit me—" and he promptly shrank to a less generous proportion. "They don't make palaces as big these days, do they?" he asked confidentially.

"They certainly do not," gulped Marcie, "Are you—are you a genie?"

"I am not," the figure said with asperity. "Can't you read? I am a djinn—Djinn Number Seven to be exact."

"Er—you mean you have to grant me my wish?"

The djinn scowled. "Now, there is a strange point of ethics," he murmured. "Since the stopper on the bottle is broken, I can't ever be shut up again. At the same time, since

you so generously let me out, I shall gladly grant you one wish. What will it be?"

Marcie didn't even hesitate. Here was a chance to make a good wedding present out of Aunt Hepsibah's nutty old bottle, and after all, she wasn't a greedy girl. She smiled brilliantly. "I'm being married in a few days—" she started.

"You want an elixir of love? Of eternal beauty?"

"No, sir-eee!" Marcie shuddered, she had read the *Arabian Nights* when she was a little girl; she knew you could not make a magical bargain with a genie—er—djinn. "No, as a matter of fact, I just want—well, a household trousseau. Nice things to be married in, and that kind of thing—just to start us off nicely."

"I'm afraid I don't quite understand." The djinn frowned, "Trousseau? That word has come in since my time. Remember, I haven't been out of this bottle since King Solomon was in diapers."

"Well—sheets, and towels, and slips, and nightgowns—" Marcie began, then dismissed it. "Oh well, just give me a dozen of everything," she told him.

"To hear is to obey," the djinn intoned. "Where shall I put it, O mistress?"

"Oh, in my room," Marcie told him, then, remembering five-dollar-a-week hall bedroom. "Maybe you'll have to enlarge the room a little, but you can do that, can't you?"

"Oh sure," said the djinn casually. "A djinn, my dear mistress, can do anything. And now, farewell forever, and thank you for letting me out."

He vanished so swiftly that Marcie rubbed her eyes, and the little cut-glass bottle fell to the floor. After a moment, Marcie picked it up, sniffing at the empty bottle. A curious faint fragrance still clung to it, but it was otherwise empty.

"Did I dream this whole thing?" she asked herself dizzily.

The buzzer rang, and the other typists in the office came back to their desks. "Gosh," someone asked, "have you been sitting here all during lunch hour, Marcie?"

"I—I took a little nap—" Marcie answered, and carefully palmed the cut-glass bottle into her desk drawer.

That afternoon seemed incredibly long to Marcie. The hands of the clock lagged as they inched around the dial, and she found herself beginning one business letter "Dear Djinn—" She ripped it out angrily, typed the date on a second letterhead, and started over; "Djinntlemen; we wish to call your attention—"

Finally, the hands reached five, and Marcie, whisking a cover over her typewriter, clutched her handbag and literally ran from the office. "There won't be anything there—" she kept telling herself, as she walked rapidly down the block, "there won't be anything—but suppose there was, suppose . . ."

The hall of the rooming house was ominously quiet. Marcie ascended the stairs, wondering at the absence of the landlady, the lack of noise from the other boarders. A curious reluctance dragged at her hands as she thrust her key into the lock.

"It's all nonsense," she said aloud. "Here goes—"

She shut her eyes and opened the door. She walked in . . .

There was a dozen of everything. The room extended into gray space, and Marcie, opening her eyes, caught her hands to her throat to stifle a scream. There were a dozen of her familiar bed; a dozen gray cats snoozing on the pillow; a dozen dainty negligees, piled carefully by it; a dozen delicate packages labeled "Nylon stockings," and a dozen red apples rolling slightly beside them. Before her staring eyes a dozen elephants lumbered through the gray space, and beyond, her terrified vision focused on a dozen white domes that faded into the dim spaces of the expanded room, and a dozen tall cathedrals as well.

A dozen of *everything* . . .

"Marcie—Marcie, where are you?" she heard a man's voice shouting from the hall. Marcie whirled. *Greg!* And he was *outside*—outside this nightmare! She fled blindly, stumbling over a dozen rolled-up Persian carpets, grazing the edge of one of a dozen grand pianos; she screamed, visualizing a dozen rattlesnakes somewhere . . .

"Greg!" she shrieked.

Twelve doors were flung violently open.

"Marcie, sweetheart, what's the matter?" pleaded a jumble of tender voices, and twelve of Greg, pushing angrily at one another, rushed into the room.

Poor Little Saturday

Madeleine L'Engle

THE WITCH WOMAN lived in a deserted, boarded-up plantation house, and nobody knew about her but me. Nobody in the nosy little town in south Georgia where I lived when I was a boy knew that if you walked down the dusty main street to where the post office ended it, and then turned left and followed that road a piece until you got to the rusty iron gates of the drive to the plantation house, you could find goings-on would make your eyes pop out. It was just luck that I found out. Or maybe it wasn't luck at all. Maybe the witch woman wanted me to find out because of Alexandra. But now I wish I hadn't because the witch woman and Alexandra are gone forever and it's much worse than if I'd never known them.

Nobody'd lived in the plantation house since the Civil War when Colonel Londermaine was killed and Alexandra Londermaine, his beautiful young wife, hung herself on the chandelier in the ballroom. A while before I was born some northerners bought it but after a few years they stopped coming and people said it was because the house was haunted. Every few years a gang of boys or men would set out to explore the house but nobody ever found anything, and it was so well boarded up it was hard to force an entrance, so by and by the town lost interest in it. No one climbed the wall and wandered around the grounds except me.

I used to go there often during the summer because I had bad spells of malaria when sometimes I couldn't bear to lie on the iron bedstead in my room with the flies buzzing around my face, or out on the hammock on the porch with the screams and laughter of the other kids as they played torturing my ears. My aching head made it impossible for me to read, and I would drag myself down the road, scuffling my bare sunburned toes in the dust, wearing the tattered straw hat that was supposed to protect me from the heat of the sun, shivering and sweating by turns. Sometimes it would seem hours before I got to the iron gates near which the brick wall was lowest. Often I would have to lie panting on the tall prickly grass for minutes until I gathered strength to scale the wall and drop down on the other side.

But once inside the grounds it seemed cooler. One funny thing about my chills was that I didn't seem to shiver nearly as much when I could keep cool as I did at home where even the walls and the floors, if you touched them, were hot. The grounds were filled with live oaks that had grown up unchecked everywhere and afforded an almost continuous green shade. The ground was covered with ferns which were soft and cool to lie on, and when I flung myself down on my back and looked up, the roof of leaves was so thick that sometimes I couldn't see the sky at all. The sun that managed to filter through lost its bright pitiless glare and came in soft yellow shafts that didn't burn you when they touched you.

One afternoon, a scorcher early in September, which is usually our hottest month (and by then you're fagged out by the heat anyhow), I set out for the plantation. The heat lay coiled and shimmering on the road. When you looked at anything through it, it was like looking through a defective pane of glass. The dirt road was so hot that it burned even through my callused feet and as I walked clouds of dust rose in front of me and mixed with the shimmying of the heat. I thought I'd never make the plantation. Sweat was running into my eyes, but it was cold sweat, and I was shivering so that my teeth chattered as I walked. When I managed finally to fling myself down on my soft green bed of ferns inside the grounds I was seized with one of the worst chills I'd ever had in spite of the fact that my mother had given me an extra dose of quinine that morning and some 666 Malaria Medicine to boot. I shut my eyes tight and clutched the ferns with my hands and teeth to wait until the chill had passed, when I heard a soft voice call:

"Boy."

I thought at first I was delirious, because sometimes I got light-headed when my bad attacks came on; only then I remembered that when I was delirious I didn't know it; all the strange things I saw and heard seemed perfectly natural. So when the voice said, "Boy," again, as soft and clear as the mockingbird at sunrise, I opened my eyes.

Kneeling near me on the ferns was a girl. She must have been about a year younger than I. I was almost sixteen so I guess she was fourteen or fifteen. She was dressed in a blue-and-white gingham dress; her face was very pale, but the kind of paleness that's supposed to be, not the sickly pale kind that was like mine showing even under the tan. Her eyes were big and very blue. Her hair was dark brown and she wore it parted in the middle in two heavy braids that were swinging in front of her shoulders as she peered into my face.

"You don't feel well, do you?" she asked. There was no trace of concern or worry in her voice. Just scientific interest.

I shook my head. "No," I whispered, almost afraid that if I talked she would vanish, because I had never seen anyone here before, and I thought that maybe I was dying because I felt so awful, and I thought maybe that gave me the power to see the ghost. But the girl in blue-and-white-checked gingham seemed as I watched her to be good flesh and blood.

"You'd better come with me," she said. "She'll make you all right."

"Who's she?"

"Oh—just Her," she said.

My chill had begun to recede by now, so when she got up off her knees, I scrambled up, too. When she stood up her dress showed a white ruffled petticoat underneath it, and bits of green moss had left patterns on her knees and I didn't think that would happen to the knees of a ghost, so I followed her as she led the way toward the house. She did not go up the sagging, half-rotted steps which led to the veranda about whose white pillars wisteria vines climbed in wild profusion, but went around to the side of the house where there were slanting doors to a cellar. The sun and rain had long since blistered and washed off the paint, but the doors looked clean and were free of the bits of bark from the eucalyptus tree which leaned nearby and which had dropped its bits of dusty peel on either side; so I knew that these cellar stairs must frequently be used.

The girl opened the cellar doors. "You go down first," she said. I went down the cellar steps, which were stone, and cool against my bare feet. As she followed me she closed the cellar doors after her and as I reached the bottom of the stairs we were in pitch darkness. I began to be very frightened until her soft voice came out of the black.

"Boy, where are you?"

"Right here."

"You'd better take my hand. You might stumble."

We reached out and found each other's hands in the darkness. Her fingers were long and cool and they closed firmly around mine. She moved with authority as though she knew her way with the familiarity born of custom.

"Poor Sat's all in the dark," she said, "but he likes it that way. He likes to sleep for weeks at a time. Sometimes he snores awfully. Sat, darling!" she called gently. A soft, bubbly, blowing sound came in answer, and she laughed happily. "Oh, Sat, you are sweet!" she said, and the bubbly sound came again. Then the girl pulled at my hand and we came out into a huge and dusty kitchen. Iron skillets, pots and pans were still hanging on either side of the huge stove, and there was a rolling pin and a bowl of flour on the marble-topped table in the middle of the room. The girl took a lighted candle off the shelf.

"I'm going to make cookies," she said as she saw me looking at the flour and the rolling pin. She slipped her hand out of mine. "Come along." She began to walk more rapidly. We left the kitchen, crossed the hall, went through the dining room, its old mahogany table thick with dust although sheets covered the pictures on the walls. Then we went into the ballroom. The mirrors lining the walls were spotted and discolored; against one wall was a single delicate gold chair, its seat cushioned with pale rose and silver-woven silk; it seemed extraordinarily well preserved. From the ceiling hung the huge chandelier from which Alexandra Londermaine had hung herself, its prisms catching and breaking up into a hundred colors the flickering of the candle and the few shafts of light that managed to slide in through the boarded-up windows. As we crossed the ball-room the girl began to dance by herself, gracefully, lightly, so that her full blue-and-white-checked gingham skirts flew out around her. She looked at herself with pleasure in the old mirrors as she danced, the candle flaring and guttering in her right hand.

"You've stopped shaking. Now what will I tell Her?" she said as we started to climb the broad mahogany staircase. It was very dark, so she took my hand again, and before we had reached the top of the stairs I obliged her by being seized by another chill. She felt my trembling fingers with satisfaction. "Oh, you've started again. That's good." She slid open one of the huge double doors at the head of the stairs.

As I looked into what once must have been Colonel Londermaine's study I thought that surely what I saw was a scene in a dream or a vision in delirium. Seated at the huge table in the center of the room was the most extraordinary woman I had ever seen. I felt that she must be very beautiful, although she would never have fulfilled any of the standards of beauty set by our town. Even though she was seated I felt that she must be immensely tall. Piled up on the table in front of her were several huge volumes, and her finger was marking the place in the open one in front of her, but she was not reading. She was leaning back in the carved chair, her head resting against a piece of blue-and-gold-embroidered silk that was flung across the chair back, one hand gently stroking a fawn that lay sleeping in her lap. Her eyes were closed and somehow I couldn't imagine what color they would be. It wouldn't have surprised me if they had been shining amber or the deep purple of her velvet robe. She had a great quantity of hair, the color of mahogany in firelight, which was cut quite short and seemed to be blown wildly about her head like flame. Under her closed eyes were deep shadows, and lines of pain about her mouth. Otherwise there were no marks of age on her face, but I would not have been surprised to learn that she was any age in the world—a hundred, or twenty-five. Her mouth was large and mobile and she was singing something in a deep, rich voice. Two cats, one black, one white, were coiled up, each on a book, and as we opened the doors a leopard stood up quietly beside her, but did not snarl or move. It simply stood there and waited, watching us.

The girl nudged me and held her finger to her lips to warn me to be quiet, but I would not have spoken—could not, anyhow, my teeth were chattering so from my chill which I had completely forgotten, so fascinated was I by this woman sitting back with her head against the embroidered silk, soft deep sounds coming out of her throat. At last these sounds resolved themselves into words, and we listened to her as she sang. The cats slept indifferently, but the leopard listened, too:

> *"I sit high in my ivory tower,*
> *The heavy curtains drawn.*
> *I've many a strange and lustrous flower,*
> *A leopard and a fawn*
>
> *"Together sleeping by my chair*
> *And strange birds softly winging,*
> *And ever pleasant to my ear*
> *Twelve maidens' voices singing.*
>
> *"Here is my magic maps' array,*
> *My mystic circle's flame.*
> *With symbol's art He lets me play,*
> *The unknown my domain,*

"And as I sit here in my dream
I see myself awake,
Hearing a torn and bloody scream,
Feeling my castle shake . . ."

Her song wasn't finished but she opened her eyes and looked at us. Now that his mistress knew we were here the leopard seemed ready to spring and devour me at one gulp, but she put her hand on his sapphire-studded collar to restrain him.

"Well, Alexandra," she said, "Who have we here?"

The girl, who still held my hand in her long, cool fingers, answered, "It's a boy."

"So I see. Where did you find him?"

The voice sent shivers up and down my spine.

"In the fern bed. He was shaking. See? He's shaking now. Is he having a fit?" Alexandra's voice was filled with pleased interest.

"Come here, boy," the woman said.

As I didn't move, Alexandra gave me a push, and I advanced slowly. As I came near, the woman pulled one of the leopard's ears gently, saying, "Lie down, Thammuz." The beast obeyed, flinging itself at her feet. She held her hand out to me as I approached the table. If Alexandra's fingers felt firm and cool, hers had the strength of the ocean and the coolness of jade. She looked at me for a long time and I saw that her eyes were deep blue, much bluer than Alexandra's, so dark as to be almost black. When she spoke again her voice was warm and tender: "You're burning up with fever. One of the malaria bugs?" I nodded. "Well, we'll fix that for you."

When she stood and put the sleeping fawn down by the leopard, she was not as tall as I had expected her to be; nevertheless she gave an impression of great height. Several

108 •

of the bookshelves in one corner were emptied of books and filled with various-shaped bottles and retorts. Nearby was a large skeleton. There was an acid-stained washbasin, too; that whole section of the room looked like part of a chemist's or physicist's laboratory. She selected from among the bottles a small amber-colored one, and poured a drop of the liquid it contained into a glass of water. As the drop hit the water there was a loud hiss and clouds of dense smoke arose. When it had drifted away she handed the glass to me and said, "Drink. Drink, my boy!"

My hand was trembling so that I could scarcely hold the glass. Seeing this, she took it from me and held it to my lips.

"What is it?" I asked.

"Drink it," she said, pressing the rim of the glass against my teeth. On the first swallow I started to choke and would have pushed the stuff away, but she forced the rest of the burning liquid down my throat. My whole body felt on fire. I felt flame flickering in every vein, and the room and everything in it swirled around. When I had regained my equilibrium to a certain extent I managed to gasp out again, "What is it?"

She smiled and answered,

> *"Nine peacocks' hearts, four bats' tongues,*
> *A pinch of moondust and a hummingbird's lungs."*

Then I asked a question I would never have dared ask if it hadn't been that I was still half drunk from the potion I had swallowed, "Are you a witch?"

She smiled again, and answered, "I make it my profession."

Since she hadn't struck me down with a flash of lightning, I went on. "Do you ride a broomstick?"

This time she laughed. "I can when I like."

"Is it—is it very hard?"

"Rather like a bucking bronco at first, but I've always been a good horsewoman, and now I can manage very nicely. I've finally progressed to sidesaddle, though I still feel safer astride. I always rode my horse astride. Still, the best witches ride sidesaddle, so . . . Now run along home. Alexandra has lessons to study and I must work. Can you hold your tongue or must I make you forget?"

"I can hold my tongue."

She looked at me and her eyes burnt into me like the potion she had given me to drink. "Yes, I think you can," she said. "Come back tomorrow if you like. Thammuz will show you out."

The leopard rose and led the way to the door. As I hesitated, unwilling to tear myself away, it came back and pulled gently but firmly on my trouser leg.

"Good-bye, boy," the witch woman said. "And you won't have any more chills and fever."

"Good-bye," I answered. I didn't say thank you. I didn't say good-bye to Alexandra. I followed the leopard out.

She let me come every day. I think she must have been lonely. After all, I was the only thing there with a life apart from hers. And in the long run the only reason I have had a life on my own is because of her. I am as much a creation of the witch woman's as Thammuz the leopard was, or the two cats, Ashtaroth and Orus (it wasn't until many years after the last day I saw the witch woman that I learned that those were the names of the fallen angels).

She did cure my malaria, too. My parents and the townspeople thought that I had outgrown it. I grew angry when they talked about it so lightly and wanted to tell them that it was the witch woman, but I knew that if ever I breathed a word about her I would be eternally damned. Mamma thought we should write a testimonial letter to the 666 Malaria Medicine people, and maybe they'd send us a couple of dollars.

Alexandra and I became very good friends. She was a strange, aloof creature. She liked me to watch her while she danced alone in the ballroom or played on an imaginary harp—though sometimes I fancied I could hear the music. One day she took me into the drawing room and uncovered a portrait that was hung between two of the long boarded-up windows. Then she stepped back and held her candle high so as to throw the best light on the picture. It might have been a picture of Alexandra herself, or Alexandra as she might be in five years.

"That's my mother," she said. "Alexandra Londermaine."

As far as I knew from the tales that went about town, Alexandra Londermaine had given birth to only one child, and that stillborn, before she had hung herself on the chandelier in the ball room—and anyhow, any child of hers would have been Alexandra's mother or grandmother. But I didn't say anything because when Alexandra got angry she became ferocious like one of the cats, and was given to leaping on me, scratching and biting. I looked at the portrait long and silently.

"You see, she has on a ring like mine," Alexandra said, holding out her left hand, on the fourth finger of which was the most beautiful sapphire-and-diamond ring I had ever seen, or rather, that I could ever have imagined, for it was a ring apart from any owned by even the most wealthy of the townsfolk. Then I realized that Alexandra had brought me in here and unveiled the portrait simply that she might show me the ring to better advantage, for she had never worn a ring before.

"Where did you get it?"

"Oh, She got it for me last night."

"Alexandra," I asked suddenly, "how long have you been here?"

"Oh, awhile."

"But how long?"

"Oh, I don't remember."

"But you must remember."

"I don't. I just came—like Poor Sat."

"Who's Poor Sat?" I asked, thinking for the first time of whoever it was that had made the gentle bubbly noises at Alexandra the day she found me in the fern bed.

"Why, we've never shown you Sat, have we!" she exclaimed. "I'm sure it's all right, but we'd better ask Her first."

So we went to the witch woman's room and knocked. Thammuz pulled the door open with his strong teeth and the witch woman looked up from some sort of experiment she was making with test tubes and retorts. The fawn, as usual, lay sleeping near her feet. "Well?" she said.

"Is it all right if I take him to see Poor Little Saturday?" Alexandra asked her.

"Yes, I suppose so," she answered. "But no teasing," and turned her back to us and bent again over her test tubes as Thammuz nosed us out of the room.

We went down to the cellar. Alexandra lit a lamp and took me back to the corner farthest from the doors, where there was a stall. In the stall was a two-humped camel. I couldn't help laughing as I looked at him because he grinned at Alexandra so foolishly, displaying all his huge buck teeth and blowing bubbles through them.

"She said we weren't to tease him," Alexandra said severely, rubbing her cheek against the preposterous splotchy hair that seemed to be coming out, leaving bald pink spots of skin on his long nose.

"But what—" I started.

"She rides him sometimes." Alexandra held out her hand while he nuzzled against it, scratching his rubbery lips against the diamond and sapphire of her ring. "Mostly She talks to him. She says he is very wise. He goes up to Her room sometimes and they talk and talk. I can't understand a word they say. She says it's Hindustani and Arabic. Sometimes I can remember little bits of it, like: *iderow, sorcabatcha,* and *anna bihed bech.* She says I can learn to speak with them when I finish learning French and Greek."

Poor Little Saturday was rolling his eyes in delight as Alexandra scratched behind his ears. "Why is he called Poor Little Saturday?" I asked.

Alexandra spoke with a ring of pride in her voice. "I named him. She let me."

"But why did you name him that?"

"Because he came last winter on the Saturday that was the shortest day of the year, and it rained all day so it got light later and dark earlier than it would have if it had been nice, so it really didn't have as much of itself as it should, and I felt so sorry for it I thought maybe it would feel better if we named him after it . . . She thought it was a nice name!" She turned on me suddenly.

"Oh, it is! It's a fine name!" I said quickly, smiling to myself as I realized how much greater was this compassion of Alexandra's for a day than any she might have for a human being. "How did she get him?" I asked.

"Oh, he just came."

"What do you mean?"

"She wanted him so he came. From the desert."

"He *walked!*"

"Yes. And swam part of the way. She met him at the beach and flew him here on the broomstick. You should have seen him. She was still all wet and looked so funny. She gave him hot coffee with things in it."

"What things?"

"Oh, just things."

Then the witch woman's voice came from behind us. "Well, children?"

It was the first time I had seen her out of her room. Thammuz was at her right heel, the fawn at her left. The cats, Ashtaroth and Orus, had evidently stayed upstairs. "Would you like to ride Saturday?" she asked me.

Speechless, I nodded. She put her hand against the wall and a portion of it slid down into the earth so that Poor Little Saturday was free to go out. "She's sweet, isn't she?" the witch woman asked me, looking affectionately at the strange, bumpy-kneed, splay-footed creature. "Her grandmother was very good to me in Egypt once. Besides, I love camel's milk."

"But Alexandra said she was a he!" I exclaimed.

"Alexandra's the kind of woman to whom all animals are he except cats, and all cats are she. As a matter of fact, Ashtaroth and Orus are she, but it wouldn't make any difference to Alexandra if they weren't. Go on out, Saturday. Come on!"

Saturday backed out, bumping her bulging knees and ankles against her stall, and stood under a live oak tree. "Down," the witch woman said. Saturday leered at me and didn't move. "Down, *sorcabatcha!*" the witch woman commanded, and Saturday obediently got down on her knees. I clambered up onto her, and before I had managed to get at all settled she rose with such a jerky motion that I knocked my chin against her front hump and nearly bit my tongue off. Round and round Saturday danced while I clung wildly to her front hump and the witch woman and Alexandra rolled on the ground with laughter. I felt as though I were on a very unseaworthy vessel on the high seas, and it wasn't long before I felt violently seasick as Saturday pranced among the live oak trees, sneezing delicately.

At last the witch woman called out, "Enough!" and Saturday stopped in her traces, nearly throwing me, and kneeling laboriously. "It was mean to tease you," the witch woman said, pulling my nose gently. "You may come sit in my room with me for a while if you like."

There was nothing I liked better than to sit in the witch woman's room and to watch her while she studied from her books, worked out strange-looking mathematical problems, argued with the zodiac, or conducted complicated experiments with her test tubes and retorts, sometimes filling the room with sulphurous odors or flooding it with red or blue light. Only once was I afraid of her, and that was when she danced with the skeleton in the corner. She had the room flooded with a strange red glow and I almost thought I could see the flesh covering the bones of the skeleton as they danced together like lovers. I think she had forgotten that I was sitting there, half hidden in the wing chair, because when they had finished dancing and the skeleton stood in the corner again, his bones shining and polished, devoid of any living trappings, she stood with her forehead against one of the deep red velvet curtains that covered the boarded-up windows and tears streamed down her cheeks. Then she went back to her test tubes and worked feverishly. She never alluded to the incident and neither did I.

As winter drew on she let me spend more and more time in the room. Once I gathered up courage enough to ask her about herself, but I got precious little satisfaction.

"Well, then, are you maybe one of the northerners who bought the place?"

"Let's leave it at that, boy. We'll say that's who I am. Did you know that my skeleton was old Colonel Londermaine? Not so old, as a matter of fact; he was only thirty-seven when he was killed at the battle of Bunker Hill—or am I getting him confused with his great-grandfather, Rudolph Londermaine? Anyhow he was only thirty-seven, and a fine figure of a man, and Alexandra only thirty when she hung herself for love of him on the chandelier in the ballroom. Did you know that the fat man with the red mustaches has been trying to cheat your father? His cow will give sour milk for seven days. Run along now and talk to Alexandra. She's lonely."

When the winter had turned to spring and the camellias and azaleas and Cape jessamine had given way to the more lush blooms of early May, I kissed Alexandra for the first time, very clumsily. The next evening when I managed to get away from the chores at home and hurried out to the plantation, she gave me her sapphire-and-diamond ring, which she had swung for me on a narrow bit of turquoise satin. "It will keep us both safe," she said, "if you wear it always. And then when we're older we can get married and you can give it back to me. Only you mustn't let anyone see it, ever, ever, or She'd be very angry."

I was afraid to take the ring but when I demurred Alexandra grew furious and started kicking and biting and I had to give in.

Summer was almost over before my father discovered the ring hanging about my neck. I fought like a witch boy to keep him from pulling out the narrow ribbon and seeing the ring, and indeed the ring seemed to give me added strength and I had grown, in any case, much stronger during the winter than I had ever been in my life. But my father was still stronger than I, and he pulled it out. He looked at it in dead silence for a moment and then the storm broke. That was the famous Londermaine ring that had disappeared the night Alexandra Londermaine hung herself. That ring was worth a fortune. Where had I got it?

No one believed me when I said I had found it in the

grounds near the house—I chose the grounds because I didn't want anybody to think I had been in the house or indeed that I was able to get in. I don't know why they didn't believe me; it still seems quite logical to me that I might have found it buried among the ferns.

It had been a long, dull year, and the men of the town were all bored. They took me and forced me to swallow quantities of corn liquor until I didn't know what I was saying or doing. When they had finished with me I didn't even manage to reach home before I was violently sick and then I was in my mother's arms and she was weeping over me. It was morning before I was able to slip away to the plantation house. I ran pounding up the mahogany stairs to the witch woman's room and opened the heavy sliding doors without knocking. She stood in the center of the room in her purple robe, her arms around Alexandra, who was weeping bitterly. Overnight the room had completely changed. The skeleton of Colonel Londermaine was gone, and books filled the shelves in the corner of the room that had been her laboratory. Cobwebs were everywhere, and broken glass lay on the floor; dust was inches thick on her work table. There was no sign of Thammuz, Ashtaroth or Orus, or the fawn, but four birds were flying about her, beating their wings against her hair.

She did not look at me or in any way acknowledge my presence. Her arm about Alexandra, she led her out of the room and to the drawing room where the portrait hung. The birds followed, flying around and around them. Alexandra had stopped weeping now. Her face was very proud and pale and if she saw me miserably trailing behind them she gave no notice. When the witch woman stood in front of the portrait the sheet fell from it. She raised her arm; there was a great cloud of smoke; the smell of sulphur filled my nostrils, and when the smoke was gone, Alexandra was gone, too. Only the portrait was there, the fourth finger of the left hand now bearing no ring. The witch woman raised her hand again and the sheet lifted itself up and covered the portrait. Then she went, with the birds, slowly back to what had once been her room, and still I tailed after, frightened as I had never been before in my life, or have been since.

She stood without moving in the center of the room for a long time. At last she turned and spoke to me.

"Well, boy, where is the ring?"

"They have it."

"They made you drunk, didn't they?"

"Yes."

"I was afraid something like this would happen when I gave Alexandra the ring. But it doesn't matter . . . I'm tired . . ." She drew her hand wearily across her forehead.

"Did I—did I tell them everything?"

"You did."

"I—I didn't know."

"I know you didn't know, boy."

"Do you hate me now?"

"No, boy, I don't hate you."

"Do you have to go away?"

"Yes."

I bowed my head. "I'm so sorry . . ."

She smiled slightly. "The sands of time . . . Cities crumble and rise and will crumble again and breath dies down and blows once more . . ."

The birds flew madly about her head, pulling at her hair, calling into her ears. Downstairs we could hear a loud pounding, and then the crack of boards being pulled away from a window.

"Go, boy," she said to me. I stood rooted, motionless, unable to move. *"Go!"* she commanded, giving me a mighty push so that I stumbled out of the room. They were waiting for me by the cellar doors and caught me as I climbed out. I had to stand there and watch when they came out with her. But it wasn't the witch woman, my witch woman. It was *their* idea of a witch woman, someone thousands of years old, a disheveled old creature in rusty black, with long wisps of gray hair, a hooked nose, and four wiry black hairs springing out of the mole on her chin. Behind her flew the four birds and suddenly they went up, up, into the sky, directly in the path of the sun until they were lost in its burning glare.

Two of the men stood holding her tightly, although she wasn't struggling, but standing there, very quiet, while the others searched the house, searched it in vain. Then as a group of them went down into the cellar I remembered, and by a flicker of the old light in the witch woman's eyes I could see that she remembered, too. Poor Little Saturday had been forgotten. Out she came, prancing absurdly up the cellar steps, her rubbery lips stretched back over her gigantic teeth, her eyes bulging with terror. When she saw the witch woman, her lord and master, held captive by two dirty, insensitive men, she let out a shriek and began to kick and lunge wildly, biting, screaming with the blood-curdling, heart-rending screams that only a camel can make. One of the men fell to the ground, holding a leg in which the bone had snapped from one of Saturday's kicks. The others scattered in terror, leaving the witch woman standing on the veranda supporting herself by clinging to one of the huge wisteria vines that curled around the columns. Saturday clambered up onto the veranda, and knelt while she flung herself between the two humps. Then off they ran, Saturday still screaming, her knees knocking together, the ground shaking as she pounded along. Down from the sun plummeted the four birds and flew after them.

Up and down I danced, waving my arms, shouting wildly until Saturday and the witch woman and the birds were lost in a cloud of dust, while the man with the broken leg lay moaning on the ground beside me.

The Fable of the Three Princes

Isaac Asimov

THERE WAS A king once named Hilderic who ruled over a very small kingdom known as Micrometrica. It was not a rich kingdom or a powerful one, but it was a happy one, because Hilderic was a good sort of king who loved his people and was loved by them.

Because Micrometrica was so small and poor, Hilderic did not try to conquer other kingdoms, and because it was so small and poor other kingdoms did not think it worthwhile to conquer it. As a result, all was peaceful and pleasant in Micrometrica.

Of course, King Hilderic didn't like to be poor. The palace was quite small, and he had to help in the garden while his wife, Queen Ermentrude, had to help in the kitchen. This made them both unhappy, but they did have an ample supply of one thing—sons.

One day, it so happened, the queen had had a child for the first time. All the kingdom would have been extremely happy, except that she overdid it. She had triplets. Three boys.

"Dear, dear," said King Hilderic, thoughtfully. "With

triplets, how will we ever decide which one shall succeed to the throne?"

"Perhaps," said Queen Ermentrude, who looked at the three new babies with love and pride, "we can allow all three to rule when the time comes."

But King Hilderic shook his head. "I don't think so, my love. The kingdom is scarcely large enough for one ruler. All the other kingdoms will laugh if it has three. Besides, what if the three should disagree? Our people would be so unhappy with quarreling monarchs."

"Well," said the queen, "we'll decide when they grow up."

The three babies grew up tall and strong and handsome, and the royal parents loved them all equally. They saw to it that all three boys studied hard, so that each one might be perfectly fit to be a king when the time came.

Though all did very well in their studies, it soon became clear that the sons were not identical triplets. Their appearances and tastes were different.

One of the three princes was larger and stronger than either of the other two. He came to be called Primus, which, in the ancient, sacred language of the kingdom, meant "number one."

When he was not at his studies, Prince Primus exercised and developed his muscles. He could lift heavy weights, bend thick iron bars, and crack a coconut in his bare hands.

Everyone in the kingdom admired his strength and thought they would feel safe if only he were the king when the time came for it.

Another son was not quite as tall or as strong as Prince Primus, and so he came to be called Secundus, which, in that same ancient, sacred language meant "number two."

His muscles didn't bulge as those of Prince Primus did,

but when he was not at his studies, he practiced with weapons of war. Prince Secundus could throw his spear farther and shoot an arrow straighter than anyone in the kingdom. No one could stand against him in a sword fight, and he rode a horse to perfection.

Everyone in the kingdom admired his skill and thought they would feel safe if he were the king, too.

The remaining son was reasonably tall and strong, but he was not quite as tall and strong as his two brothers, so he was named Tertius, which meant "number three."

Prince Tertius was even better at his studies than his two brothers, but he was not interested in lifting weights or throwing spears. When he was not studying, he wrote love poems and would sing them in a very pleasant voice. He also read a great many books.

The young ladies of the kingdom thought the poetry of Prince Tertius was beautiful. Everyone else, however, wasn't sure it would be safe to have a poet as king. They were glad there were two stronger princes to choose from.

The three princes were quite friendly with each other, fortunately, and as they grew older, they decided that they would not fight or quarrel over who was to be the king someday. In fact, they loved their father and wanted him to stay king for many years.

"Still," said Prince Primus, "Our Royal Father is getting old, and we must come to some decision. Since we are all the same age there's no use trying to select the oldest. However, I am the largest and strongest. There's that to consider."

"Yes," said Prince Secundus, "but I am the most skilled warrior. I don't want to make a fuss about that, but it is important."

"I think," said Prince Tertius, "we ought to let Dad and Mom make the decision."

Prince Primus frowned. "I don't think you ought to call Our Royal Parents 'Dad and Mom.' "

"But that's who they are," said Prince Tertius.

"That is not the point," said Prince Secundus. "There is their dignity to think of. If I were king someday, I should certainly expect you to refer to me as 'My Royal Brother.' I should be very hurt if you were to call me 'buddy' or 'pal.' "

"That is very true," said Prince Primus. "If I were king, I would despise being referred to in a casual manner."

"In that case," said Tertius, who never liked to quarrel, "why don't we ask Our Royal Parents what we ought to do? After all, they are the monarchs, and we should obey their wishes."

"Very well," said the other two, and all three rushed to the royal throne room.

King Hilderic thought about it. Being a good king, he wanted to do what was best for his little country. He wasn't at all sure that the country would be well off under a very strong king, or a very warlike king, or even a very poetic king.

What the country needed, he thought, was a very *rich* king, one who could spend money to make the country happier and more prosperous.

Finally he sighed, and said, "There's no way I can choose among you. I will have to send you on a hard and dangerous quest to get money—a great deal of money. I don't want to make it seem that money is so terribly important, but, you know, we *do* need it quite badly. Therefore the one who brings back the most money will be king."

Queen Ermentrude looked very disturbed. "But, Father—" (She never called him "Your Majesty" unless courtiers were about, and the kingdom was so poor there weren't

126 •

many of those.) "But, Father," she said, "what if our dear princes should be hurt in the course of the quest?"

"We can only hope they won't be hurt, Mother, but we need money, you see, and Emperor Maximian of Allemania has a great deal of money. He is probably the richest monarch in the world."

Prince Primus said, "That may be so, My Royal Father, but the emperor won't give us money just because we ask for it."

Prince Secundus said, "In fact, no one will give us money just because we ask for it."

Prince Tertius said, "I don't think princes ought to ask for money in any case."

"Well, my princes," said the king, "it is not a matter of asking for money. The Emperor Maximian, it seems, has a daughter named Meliversa. She is an only child."

He put on a large pair of spectacles and pulled a stiff sheet of parchment from a drawer in the royal desk.

He said, "I received this notice by courier two days ago, and I have been studying it ever since. It has been distributed to all the kings in the world, and it is really very kind of the emperor to remember me, since I am king of so small and poor a country."

He cleared his throat. "It says here," he said, glancing over the parchment very carefully, "that the imperial princess is as beautiful as the day; tall, slender, and very well educated."

Prince Primus said, "It's a little troublesome to have a princess well educated. She may talk too much."

"But we needn't listen to her," said Prince Secundus.

Prince Tertius said, "But, My Royal Father, what has the imperial princess got to do with the matter of obtaining money?"

"Well, my young princes," said the king, "anyone who is a

royal prince, and who can prove he is one by presenting his birth certificate, will be allowed to demonstrate his abilities. If these should please the imperial princess Meliversa so that she wishes to marry the prince, he will be named successor to the throne and given a large allowance. Then, eventually, he will become emperor. If it is one of you, why then he will also become king of this country in time; and with the wealth of the empire to dispose of, he will make Micrometrica very prosperous."

Prince Primus said, "The Princess Meliversa could never resist my muscles, My Royal Father."

Prince Secundus said, "Or my horsemanship, if it comes to that."

Prince Tertius said, "I wonder if she likes poetry. . . ."

King Hilderic said, "There is one catch though. I have educated you boys in economics, sociology, and other subjects a king must know. Meliversa, however, has been educated in sorcery. If any prince tries to win her heart and fails, she will turn him into a statue. She says she needs a great many statues for the promenade in her park."

Queen Ermentrude said, "I knew it," and began to weep.

"Don't weep, My Royal Mother," said Prince Tertius, who loved her dearly. "I'm sure it isn't legal to turn princes into statues."

"Not ordinarily," said the king, "but it is part of the agreement. Besides, it is difficult to argue law with an imperial princess. So if you princes don't want to take the chance, I certainly won't blame you. . . . It's just that we need money so badly."

Prince Primus said, "I am not afraid. She will never be able to resist me."

"Or me," said Prince Secundus.

Prince Tertius looked thoughtful and said nothing.

The three princes made ready at once for the long journey. Their clothing was rather faded and out of fashion, and their horses were old, but that was all they could manage.

"Farewell, My Royal Parents," said Prince Primus. "I shall not fail you."

"I hope not," said King Hilderic doubtfully, while Queen Ermentrude wept quietly in the background.

"I shall not fail you either, My Royal Parents," said Prince Secundus.

Prince Tertius waited for the other two to start on the way, and then he said, "Good-bye, Mom and Dad. I will do my best."

"Good-bye, son," said King Hilderic, who had a lump in his throat.

Queen Ermentrude hugged Prince Tertius, who then galloped after his two brothers.

It took the three princes a long time to reach the chief city of the empire. Their horses were very tired by then, and their clothes were quite worn out. They had also used up their money and had had to borrow from the treasurers of the kingdoms through which they passed.

"So far," said Prince Tertius sadly, "we've piled up a considerable debt, which makes our kingdom worse off than ever."

"After I've won the princess," said Prince Primus, "I will pay the debt three times over."

"I will pay it five times over," said Prince Secundus.

Prince Tertius said, "That's *if* one of us wins."

"How can we lose?" asked Princes Primus and Secundus together.

And indeed, when they arrived in the capital, they were greeted with kindness. They were given fresh horses and beautiful new clothing of the richest description, and were shown to a lavish suite in the largest and most beautiful palace they had ever imagined. Many servants were at their call, and all served them with the greatest politeness.

The three princes were very pleased with their treatment.

Prince Primus said, "The emperor must know what a wonderful family we come from. Our ancestors have been kings for many generations."

"Yes," said Prince Tertius, "but they have all been poor kings. I wonder if the Emperor Maximian knows that."

"He must," said Prince Secundus. "Emperors know everything. Otherwise, how could they be emperors?"

The second-assistant servingmaid was at that moment bringing in fresh towels so that the princes might take their baths in preparation for a great feast that night.

Prince Primus said at once, "You! Servingmaid!"

The servingmaid trembled at being addressed by a prince, and curtsied very low. "Yes, Your Highness."

"Is the emperor a wise emperor?"

The servingmaid said, "Oh, Your Highness, the entire empire marvels at his wisdom."

Prince Secundus said, "Would he care whether the princes who visit him are rich or poor?"

"Oh no, Your Highness," said the servingmaid. "He is so wealthy that money means nothing to him. He is concerned only with the happiness of his daughter. If she asks to marry a certain prince, that prince will become heir to the kingdom even if he doesn't possess a single penny."

Prince Primus and Prince Secundus smiled and nodded to each other as though to say: We knew it all along.

Prince Tertius smiled at the servingmaid and said, "And what about the princess, my dear? Is she as pretty as you are?"

The servingmaid turned very pink and her mouth fell open. She seemed quite unable to speak.

Prince Primus said to his brother in a low voice, "Don't

call her 'my dear.' It unsettles servants to be addressed so by a prince."

Prince Secundus said to his brother in an even lower voice, "How can a servingmaid be pretty? A servingmaid is just a servingmaid."

Prince Tertius said, "Just the same, I would like an answer to my question."

The servingmaid, who was really quite pretty even though she was a servingmaid (but most princes wouldn't have noticed that), said, "Your Royal Highness must be joking. The princess is taller than I am and far more beautiful. She is as beautiful as the sun."

"Ah," said Prince Primus. "A rich princess who is as beautiful as the sun is someone to be interested in."

Prince Secundus said, "It would be quite a pleasure to have a rich princess like that about one's palace."

Prince Tertius said, "She might be too bright to look at, if she is as beautiful as the sun."

The servingmaid said, "But she is haughty."

Prince Primus said at once, "A servingmaid may not speak unless she is spoken to."

Prince Secundus said severely, "This comes of saying 'my dear' to servingmaids."

But Prince Tertius said, "Is she *very* haughty, my dear?"

"*Very* haughty, Your Highness," said the servingmaid, trembling at the haughty stares of the other two brothers. "There have been a number of princes who have already applied for her hand, but she would have none of them."

"Of course not," said Prince Primus. "They were probably pipsqueaks who couldn't bend an iron bar an inch. Why should she be interested in them?"

"Probably," said Prince Secundus, "they couldn't even lift a sword, let alone fight with one. She wouldn't be interested in them."

"Perhaps," said Prince Tertius, "we ought to ask the servingmaid what became of the princes who didn't please the princess."

The servingmaid's eyes dropped, and she said sadly, "They were all turned into statues, Your Highness. Handsome statues, for they were all young and handsome princes."

Prince Tertius shook his head. "I had hoped the emperor was only joking, but he must have really meant what he said on the parchment. Are there many of those statues?"

"There are about a dozen on each side of the garden path along which the princess walks each morning, Your Highness. She never looks at them, for she is as hard-hearted as she is beautiful."

"Pooh," said Prince Primus. "It doesn't matter that she is hard-hearted, as long as she is rich. And beautiful, too, of course. I shall soften her heart. . . . Now be off with you at once, servingmaid."

The servingmaid curtsied deeply and left the room, taking backward steps, for it would have been very impolite for her to turn her back on three princes.

That night there was a great feast, and the three princes were the guests of honor.

The emperor, seated on a splendid throne at the head of the table, greeted them. Next to him was the Princess Meliversa, and she was indeed as beautiful as the sun. Her hair was long and the color of corn silk. Her eyes were blue and reminded everyone of the sky on a bright spring day. Her features were perfectly regular and her skin was flawless.

But her eyes were empty, and her face was expressionless.

She did not smile when Prince Primus was introduced to her. She looked at him proudly and said, "What kingdom are you from?"

He said, "I am from Micrometrica, Your Imperial Highness."

The princess said with contempt, "I know all the kingdoms of Earth, and Micrometrica is the smallest of them." And she looked away from him.

Prince Primus backed away from her and took his seat at the table. He whispered to Prince Tertius, "She will grow interested once I show her what I can do."

Prince Secundus was introduced to her, and she said, "You are also from Micrometrica, I imagine."

"Yes, Your Imperial Highness. Prince Primus is my brother."

"Micrometrica is also the poorest kingdom on Earth. If you and your brother must share its wealth, you must be poor indeed." And she looked away from him.

Prince Secundus backed away from her and took his seat at the table. He whispered to Prince Tertius, "She will forget our poverty when I show her what I can do."

Prince Tertius was introduced to her, and she said, "Still another from Micrometrica?"

"We are triplets, Your Imperial Highness," said Prince Tertius, "though not identical ones. And what we have, we share."

"But you have nothing to share."

"We have no money and no power," said Prince Tertius, "but we and our kingdom are happy. And when happiness is shared, it increases."

"I have never noticed that," said the princess, and she looked away from him.

Prince Tertius backed away from her and took his seat at the table. He whispered to his brothers, "She is rich, and our country needs money. But her beauty is ice-cold and her wealth does not bring her happiness."

The next morning Prince Primus made ready to put on a demonstration of his abilities for the princess. He had dressed in a fine pair of athletic shorts supplied by the emperor, and he made his magnificent muscles ripple as he stood before the mirror. He was quite satisfied with his appearance.

At that moment, however, there was a timid knock on the door, and when Prince Primus called, "Enter," the second-assistant servingmaid came in with a bowl of apples.

"What is this?" demanded Prince Primus.

The servingmaid said, "I thought you might wish some refreshment before undertaking your task, Your Highness."

"Nonsense," said Prince Primus. "I have all the refreshment I need. Take away those silly apples."

"I also wonder, Your Highness," said the servingmaid, blushing at her own daring in continuing to speak to him, "if you ought to undertake the task."

"Why not?" said Prince Primus, flexing his arms and smiling at himself in the mirror. "Do you think I am not manly enough?"

The servingmaid said, "You are certainly manly enough for anyone in the world but the princess. She is so hard to please, and it would be a shame that such a fine prince as Your Highness should be made into a marble statue."

Prince Primus laughed scornfully. "She cannot be so hard to please that *I* do not please her—and that is enough talk. You must only speak when spoken to, servingmaid. Get out at once."

And the servingmaid got out at once, though she curtsied first.

Prince Primus stepped out into the large arena. Before him were the stands, covered by a beautiful silk canopy. The emperor was seated in the center, and at his right was the imperial Princess Meliversa. The officials of the court were in the stands too, as were many a young gentleman and young lady. In one corner were Prince Secundus and Prince Tertius.

Prince Primus faced the stands, and around him was all the equipment he needed.

He turned, to begin with, to a large stack of barbells. The lighter ones he tossed aside lightly, even though an ordinary man might have had trouble lifting them.

Then he lifted the heavier ones, seizing them with both hands and bringing them up to his shoulders with a jerk, and then, more slowly, lifting them high in the air.

All the courtiers broke into applause when he managed to lift the heaviest weight that had been supplied. No other person had ever been known to lift that weight.

Finally he bent an iron bar by placing it behind his neck and pulling the ends forward till they met in front of him. He then pulled the ends apart again, lifted the bar over his head, and threw it to one side.

Whatever he did brought round after round of applause from the courtiers. Even the emperor nodded approvingly. The princess, however, did not applaud; nor did she nod.

The emperor bent toward his daughter and said, "Really, my dear, this prince is quite the strongest man I have ever seen. It would be a pretty good thing to make him heir to the throne."

The princess said coldly, "It would be a pretty good thing to make him a strong man at the circus, My Imperial Father, but he is quite unsuitable for marriage to me. After all, do I have a set of weights in my chamber, or iron bars that need bending? I would quickly grow weary of watching him flex his arms, and if he tried to embrace me, he would break my ribs."

She rose in her seat, and at once everyone was quiet.

"Prince Primus," she said in her beautiful voice.

Prince Primus folded his arms and listened confidently.

The princess said, "You are the strongest man I have ever seen, and I thank you for your efforts to please me. However, I do not wish you for my husband. You know the penalty."

She made a mystic pass with her hands (for she was a very well-educated princess indeed), and there was a bright flash of light. The courtiers had covered their eyes, for they knew what to expect; but Prince Secundus and Prince Tertius were not prepared, and they were blinded for a moment by the flash.

When they recovered, they saw a statue being loaded into a cart so that it might be transported to the avenue in the garden along which the princess took her morning walk.

The statue was that of Prince Primus, arms folded, expression handsome and proud.

Prince Tertius was sad that evening. He had never lost a brother before, and he found he didn't like it.

He said to Prince Secundus, "I think Our Royal Parents will be terribly distressed. How are we going to tell them?"

Prince Secundus said, "After I win the princess's hand, I may perhaps be able to persuade her to try to find a way to restore Our Royal Brother. After all, someone as well educated as she ought to be able to think of a way of doing so."

"But how will you be able to win her hand? She seems to have a heart of stone. Cold stone."

"Not at all," said Prince Secundus. "It's just that she wasn't interested in useless strength and muscles. What good is it to lift weights? Now *I* am a warrior. I can fight and handle weapons. That is a useful occupation."

"I hope so," said Prince Tertius, "but you will be taking a

great chance. Still, the princess is rich, and we *do* need the money."

The next morning Prince Secundus was arraying himself in gleaming armor when the second-assistant servingmaid staggered in, carrying an enormous sword for him. She was bowed down by its weight, and when she tried to curtsy, she dropped it with a loud clang.

Prince Secundus said with annoyance, "You are very clumsy."

"I beg your pardon, Your Highness," she said humbly, curtsying again, "but are you really going to undertake the task for the princess?"

"Certainly I am, but what business is that of yours, servingmaid?"

"None at all, Your Highness," admitted the servingmaid, "but the princess is so hard-hearted and so difficult to please. I do not want to see you turned into a statue, like your brother."

"I will not be turned into a statue," said Prince Secundus, "because the princess will be fascinated with me. And now, servingmaid, leave my presence at once. I cannot bear anyone as impertinent as you are."

The servingmaid curtsied and left.

Prince Secundus stepped out into the arena, and at once there was applause from all the courtiers. The armor that had been given him by the emperor was beautiful and shiny, and fit him very well. His shield was pure white, his sword was of the best steel, his spear was perfectly balanced, and his helmet covered his face and gave him a ferocious appearance.

He threw his spear, and it flew the length of the arena and impaled itself in the center of a target.

Prince Secundus then challenged anyone at all to a sword fight. A large man in armor came into the arena, and for long minutes the two fought, sword clashing on shield. But Prince Secundus could strike twice for every once that his opponent could, and as the other tired, Prince Secundus seemed to grow stronger. Soon enough, the opponent raised his hands in surrender, and Prince Secundus was the victor. The applause was deafening.

Finally Prince Secundus removed his helmet and armor and mounted a horse. With one hand only, he controlled the horse perfectly, making it rear on its hind legs, leap, and dance. It was a remarkable performance, and the audience went wild.

"Really, my dear," said the emperor, as he bent toward his daughter, "this prince is an excellent warrior. He could lead my armies into battle and defeat all my enemies. Surely he must please you."

The princess's haughty face was cold, and she said, "He might make an excellent general if he also knew how to handle an army, but of what use would he be as a husband? There are no armed men in my chamber for him to fight, no horses for him to ride, no targets for him to shoot at. And if he forgot himself, he might throw his spear at me, since weapons are his greatest love and talent."

She rose in her seat, and at once everyone was quiet. She said, "Prince Secundus, you are the greatest warrior I have ever seen, and I thank you for your efforts to please me. However, I do not wish you for my husband. You know the penalty."

She made the same mystic pass as before. This time Prince Tertius knew enough to cover his eyes. When he took his hand away, there was another statue: that of a graceful, handsome prince with one hand raised as though it had just

• 139

hurled a spear. Prince Tertius knew that he had lost a second brother.

Prince Tertius sat alone in the suite the next morning. He hadn't slept all night, and to tell the truth, he didn't know what to do.

He said to himself, "If I go home now, everyone will say I am a coward. Besides, how can I go home now and break the news to Dad? And dear Mom will weep for the rest of her life. As for me, I have lost two brothers who were good brothers to me, even if they were a little conceited and headstrong."

And now the second-assistant servingmaid edged her way into the room. She had nothing in her hands.

Prince Tertius said, "Are you bringing me something, my dear?"

She curtsied very nervously and said, "No, Your Highness. Do not be angry with me, for I have only come to tell you that I asked both your brothers not to attempt the task, but they would not listen."

Prince Tertius sighed. "They were both very willful, I know. You mustn't blame yourself that they did not listen to you. And certainly I am not angry with you."

"Then, Your Highness, would *you* listen to me if I ask you not to attempt the task? You are not a great strongman or a great warrior. How can you win the cold, hard princess if your brothers could not?"

Prince Tertius said, "I know that all I can do is write a little poetry and sing a bit, but perhaps the princess might like that."

"She is very hard to please, Your Highness," said the servingmaid, shuddering at her impudence in arguing with a prince. "If you are made into a statue too, your parents will

140 •

be left entirely without children, and they will have no heir to the throne."

Prince Tertius sighed again. "You are perfectly correct, little servingmaid. You have a kind heart and a thoughtful mind. But you see, our kingdom is so poor that Dad has to help in the garden and Mom has to help in the kitchen. If I could marry the princess, I would become so rich that I could make Mom and Dad and the whole kingdom happy. . . . So I think I *must* try to please the princess. Perhaps if I use my very best poems and sing them as sweetly as I can, she will be pleased."

Tears rolled down the servingmaid's cheeks. "Oh, how I wish she would, but she is so hard-hearted. If only she had *my* heart inside her, it would be different."

"Well then, my dear," said Prince Tertius, "let me test your heart. I will sing you some of my songs, and you can tell me if *you* like them. If you do, perhaps the princess will like them too."

The servingmaid was horrified, "Oh, Your Highness. You mustn't do that. Your songs are made to be sung to a princess, not to a simple servingmaid. How can you judge a princess by a servingmaid?"

"In that case," said Prince Tertius, "let us forget the princess, and I will ask only what the servingmaid thinks."

Prince Tertius tuned his lyre, one that was his own and that he had brought with him. Then, in a very soft and melodious voice, he sang a sad song of love denied. And when the servingmaid seemed to melt away in tears at the sadness, he sang a happy song of love attained, so that the tears vanished and she clapped her hands and laughed.

"Did you like them?" said Prince Tertius.

"Oh yes," said the servingmaid. "The songs were beautiful, and your voice made me feel as though I were in heaven."

• 141

Prince Tertius smiled. "Thank you, my lady." He bent and kissed her hand, and the servingmaid turned red with confusion and quickly put the hand he had kissed behind her back.

But just then there was a loud knock on the door, and there entered a chamberlain, a high court official, who bowed to Prince Tertius (but not very deeply) and said, "Your Highness, the imperial Princess Meliversa wishes to know why you have not appeared in the arena."

He looked hard at the second-assistant servingmaid as he said this, and the terrified young woman left the room hurriedly.

Prince Tertius said, "I do not know whether I will undertake the task. I am considering it."

The chamberlain bowed even less deeply than before and said, "I will inform the princess of what you have said. Please remain in this room until she decides what is to be done."

Prince Tertius waited in the room and wondered if the princess would turn him into a statue at once for hesitating over the task.

He was still wondering about it when the princess Meliversa entered the room. She did not knock. Imperial princesses never knock.

She said, "My chamberlain tells me that you might not undertake the task."

Prince Tertius said, "Your Imperial Highness may not like my poetry or my voice. It is all I have to offer."

"But if I do like them, what then?"

"In that case, I wonder if I wish to have as my wife someone who is so cold and hard-hearted, she is willing to turn brave, good princes into statues."

"Am I not beautiful, Prince?"

• 143

"It is an outside beauty, Imperial Princess."

"Am I not rich, Prince?"

"Only in money, Imperial Princess."

"Are you not poor, Prince?"

"Only in money, Imperial Princess, and I am used to it, actually, as are my parents and my kingdom."

"Do you not wish to be rich, Prince, by marrying me?"

"I think not, Imperial Princess. I am, after all, not for sale."

"And yet my chamberlain, on the other side of your door, heard you singing to a low-born servingmaid."

"That is true, but the servingmaid was tender-hearted and loving, and I wanted to sing to her. A tender and loving heart is, after all, the beauty and wealth I really want. If she will have me, then I will marry her, and someday, when I am king in my father's place, the low-born servingmaid will be my queen."

At that, the princess smiled. She was even more beautiful when she smiled. "Now," she said, "you will see the use of a good education."

She made a motion with her hand, muttered two or three words, and with that she grew foggy in appearance, shrunk a little, changed a little—and Prince Tertius found himself looking at the second-assistant servingmaid.

He said in amazement, "Which are you, the imperial princess or the servingmaid?"

She said, "I am both, Prince Tertius. It was in the form of a servingmaid that I set myself the task of finding a suitable husband. Of what use was it to me what princes might do to win the hand of a beautiful and rich princess, not caring that she was cold and cruel. What I wanted was someone who would be kind and loving to a gentle, tender-hearted girl, even if she was not as beautiful as the sun or richer than gold. You have passed that test."

Again she changed and was the princess again, but a smiling, warm princess.

"Will you have me as wife now, Prince Tertius?"

And Prince Tertius said, "If you will remain always in your heart the gentle, loving woman I came to love, then I will marry you."

And with that all the princes who had been statues were suddenly brought back to warm flesh and blood again.

Prince Tertius and Princess Meliversa were married two months later, after the king and queen of Micrometrica were brought to the Imperial City by the very fastest coaches. They were as happy as anyone can imagine.

Prince Primus and Prince Secundus were also as happy as anyone can imagine, for they were alive again instead of being frozen in cold stone. They kept saying, "The servingmaid? We would never have imagined such a thing!"

Naturally, Prince Tertius was happy too, but the imperial princess was happiest of all. After all, she had been afraid that even with all her education she would never find anyone who would turn away from mere beauty and money, and love her for herself alone.

Letters from Camp

Al Sarrantonio

Dear Mom and Dad,

I still don't know why you made me come to this dump for the summer. It looks like all the other summer camps I've been to, even if it is "super modern and computerized," and I don't see why I couldn't go back to the one I went to last year instead of this "new" one. I had a lot of fun last summer, even if you did have to pay for all that stuff I smashed up and even if I did make the head counselor break his leg.

The head counselor here is a jerk, just like the other one was. As soon as we got off the hovercraft that brought us here, we had to go to the Big Tent for a "pep talk." They made us sit through a slide show about all the things we're going to do (yawn), and that wouldn't have been so bad except that the head counselor, who's a robot, kept scratching his metal head through the whole thing. I haven't made any friends, and the place looks like it's full of jerks. Tonight we didn't have any hot water and the TV in my tent didn't work.

Phooey on Camp Ultima. Can't you still get me back in the other place?

Dear Mom and Dad,

Maybe this place isn't so bad after all. They just about let us do whatever we want, and the kids are pretty wild. Today they split us up into "Pow-wow Groups," but there aren't really any rules or anything, and my group looks like it might be a good one. One of the guys in it looks like he might be okay. His name's Ramon, and he's from Brazil. He told me a lot of neat stories about things he did at home, setting houses on fire and things like that. We spent all day today hiding from our stupid robot counselor. He thought for sure we had run away, and nearly blew a circuit until we finally showed up just in time for dinner.

The food stinks, but they did have some animal-type thing that we got to roast over a fire, and that tasted pretty good.

Tomorrow we go on our first field trip.

Dear Mom and Dad,

We had a pretty good time today, all things considered. We got up at six o'clock to go on our first hike, and everybody was pretty excited. There's a lot of wild places here, and they've got it set up to look just like a prehistoric swamp. One kid said we'd probably see a Tyrannosaurus Rex, but nobody believed him. The robot counselors kept us all together as we set out through the marsh, and we saw a lot of neat things like vines dripping green goop and all kinds of frogs and toads. Me and Ramon started pulling the legs off frogs, but our counselor made us stop and anyway the frogs were all robots. We walked for about two hours and then stopped for lunch. Then we marched back again.

The only weird thing that happened was that when we got back and the counselors counted heads, they found that one kid was missing. They went out to look for him but couldn't find anything, and the only thing they think might have happened is that he got lost in the bog somewhere. One kid said he thought he saw a Tyrannosaurus Rex, but it was the same kid who'd been talking about them before so nobody listened to him. The head counselor went around patting everybody on the shoulder, telling us not to worry since something always happens to one kid every year. But they haven't found him yet.

Tonight we had a big food fight, and nobody even made us clean the place up.

Dear Mom and Dad,

Today we went out on another field trip, and another stupid kid got himself lost. They still haven't found the first one, and some of the kids are talking about Tyrannosaurus Rex again. But this time we went hill climbing and I think the dope must have fallen off a cliff, because the hills are almost like small mountains and there are a lot of ledges on them.

After dinner tonight, which almost nobody ate because nobody felt like it, we sat around a campfire and told ghost stories. Somebody said they thought a lot of kids were going to disappear from here, and that made everybody laugh, in a scary kind of way. I was a little scared myself. It must have been the creepy shadows around the fire. The robot counselors keep telling everyone not to worry, but some of the kids—the ones who can't take it—are starting to say they want to go home.

I don't want to go home, though; this place is fun.

Dear Mom and Dad,

Today we went on another trip, to the far side of the island where they have a lake, and we had a good time and all (we threw one of the robot counselors into the lake but he didn't sink), but when we got off the boat and everybody was counted we found out that eight kids were gone. One kid said he even saw his friend Harvey get grabbed by something ropy and black and pulled over the side. I'm almost ready to believe him. I don't know if I like this place so much any more. One more field trip like the one today and I think I'll want to come home.

It's not even fun wrecking stuff around here any more.

Dear Mom and Dad,

Come and get me right away, I'm *scared.* Today the robot counselors tried to make us go on another day trip, but nobody wanted to go, so we stayed around the tents. But at the chow meeting tonight only twelve kids showed up. That means twenty more kids disappeared today. Nobody had any idea what happened to them, though I do know that a whole bunch of guys were playing outside the perimeter of the camp, tearing things down, so that might have had something to do with it. At this point I don't care.

Just get me out of here!

Mom and Dad,

I think I'm the only kid left, and I don't know if I can hide much longer. The head counselor tricked us into leaving the camp today, saying that somebody had seen a Tyrannosaurus Rex. He told us all to run through the rain forest at the north end of the camp, but when we ran into it, something horrible happened. I was with about five other kids, and as soon as we ran into the forest we heard a high-pitched screeching and a swishing sound and the trees above us started to lower their branches. I saw four of the kids I was with get covered by green plastic-looking leaves, and then there was a gulping sound and the branches lifted and separated and there was nothing there. Ramon and I just managed to dodge out of the way, and we ran through the forest

in between the trees and out the other side. We would have been safe for a while but just then the robot counselors broke through the forest behind us, leading a Tyrannosaurus Rex. We ran, but Ramon slipped and fell and the Tyrannosaurus Rex was suddenly there, looming over him with its dripping jaws and rows of sharp white teeth. Ramon took out his box of matches but the dinosaur was on him then and I didn't wait to see any more.

I ran all the way back to the postal computer terminal in the camp to get this letter out to you. Call the police! Call the army! I can't hide forever, and I'm afraid that any second the Tyrannosaurus Rex will break in here and

Dear Mr. and Mrs. Jameson:

Camp Ultima is happy to inform you of the successful completion of your son's stay here, and we are therefore billing you for the balance of your payment at this time.

Camp Ultima is proud of its record of service to parents of difficult boys, and will strive in the future to continue to provide the very best in camp facilities.

May we take this opportunity to inform you that, due to the success of our first camp, we are planning to open a new facility for girls next summer.

We hope we might be of service to you in the future.

Things That Go Quack in the Night

Lewis and Edith Shiner

THE NOTE WAS stuck to the refrigerator with one of those little round magnets, so I'd be sure to see it when I got home from school. It read:

> My dearest son—
>
> I only wish I could explain this all to you, but I know you wouldn't believe me. So I'll just say that I have to go away. I'll probably never be back. I'm fine, and I love you, but it's just something I have to do.
>
> Love,
Mom
>
> P.S. Remember, don't feed the goldfish more than once a week or they'll bloat.

I'd grown up without a father, and now, only a few days before my eighteenth birthday, I'd lost my mother as well. Someone else might have reacted with grief or despair, but frankly, it made me a little angry. I swore I would find her and at least make her tell me the reason she'd gone.

She'd left most of her belongings behind, and I went through all of them, looking for a clue. Finally, stuffed into the toe of an old pair of hiking boots, I found the following letter:

> Dear Emily,
>   So good to hear from you after all these years, and with such good news as well! I look forward to seeing you and Jonathan, and of course, in the circumstances, you're welcome to stay as long as you choose.
>
> > Fondly,
> > Dr. Canard

The letter was little more than a week old, which was pretty strange, considering that Jonathan was my father's name and he was supposed to have died before I was even born. The letterhead read "the clinic," just like that, with the fashionable lower-case letters, and gave an address in Switzerland.

I was very interested in learning the "circumstances" that the mysterious Dr. Canard had referred to.

"The clinic" sat on top of a pine- and cedar-coated hill that looked down on Lake Zurich. My nerves were still shaky from a ride across the lake in a suspended cable car that we called a Swiss Sky Ride in America, but which the Swiss seemed to think was some kind of public transportation.

It was a beautiful setting, real picture-postcard stuff, but I was in no mood for it. It's not that easy to go jetting around the world when you're only seventeen, particularly when the police are still trying to puzzle out why your mother disappeared.

I went right up to the front door and rang the bell under

the little brass plaque with Canard's name on it. I didn't hear anything inside, but a moment later a woman opened the door. She was wearing the kind of uniform that French maids wear in cartoons that I'm not supposed to be old enough for.

"I'm here to see Dr. Canard," I said, and she led me into a room with big leather chairs, a fireplace, and a rear wall full of windows. An old man wearing a monocle and jodhpurs sat in one of the chairs. His mass of fine white hair was uncombed, and his goatee was just a little off-center.

When he saw me, the monocle popped right out of his head.

"That will be all, Joseph," he said to the maid. I took another look at her and saw what might have been a light stubble around the chin.

"Very good, Doctor," the maid said in a deep voice, and turned away. I settled uncomfortably into one of the chairs.

"And you," he said, looking me over, "you would be Drake Russel, *nicht wahr?*"

I started to answer him but didn't get the chance. "I'm glad to see you. How glad are you, Canard?" he asked himself, plowing right ahead without giving me an opening. "So glad that I shall offer you some tea. Would you like some tea? Of course you would."

Dr. Canard, I realized, was a loony.

He poured a cup of tea, then left it sitting on the trolley while he walked over to a long sliding glass door. On the slope outside two of the largest mallards I'd ever seen in my life were waddling toward us, gesturing with their bills and wagging their stubby tails. Canard suddenly pulled a cord, and curtains shot out to cover the glass.

The room fell into near-darkness, and I wrestled with an urge to run away before things got any stranger.

"You are here," Canard said, "to ask about your parents,

nicht wahr? Of course you are. But why should I tell you? You would not believe me."

"Why don't you—"

"And why wouldn't he, Canard? Is he not an intelligent lad? Clear-eyed, bright-cheeked? Very well then. I shall tell you. But you must pay attention, and you must not interrupt."

I was going to tell him that there didn't seem to be much chance of that, but he had already started his story.

On their honeymoon, Jonathan and Emily Russel came to the Hotel Anatidae, a secluded resort on Lake Zurich. They had been married a little over a day and had just finished dinner in the hotel's elegant and somewhat overpriced restaurant.

Things, as things should be on a honeymoon, were quite nearly perfect. They had scoffed at the waiter's warnings that they should return to their cabin before dark, lingering instead over a second bottle of wine.

"Just what is it," Jonathan had finally asked him, "that you think is going to happen to us?"

"There are things in the night," the waiter intoned solemnly, "that you Americans know nothing of."

"Such as?" Jonathan demanded. "Muggers? Here?" He and Emily both laughed.

"Beware," the waiter had told them. "I can say no more."

The full moon was rising as they strolled, hand in hand, along the lake. Emily had saved a crust of bread from the table and was distributing it among a gaggle of ducks that had waddled after them across the lawn.

"What do you call an incompetent doctor?" she asked them.

"Quack!"

"Right!" She threw a piece to one of them. "What do you call a break in the sidewalk?"

"Quack?"

"Very good!"

A huge mallard, well over two feet tall, had joined the throng. His bill was bright orange, and the moonlight glistened off the green on his wings. Strong and proud a specimen as it was, Jonathan still found something odd, almost human, in the animal's expression.

"Give me some of that bread, will you?" he asked his wife. He held out a chunk of bread toward the duck. "Here, old boy, would you like—"

The duck moved with startling swiftness. "Ouch!" Jonathan cried, as the bread disappeared and a stab of pain went through his hand.

"What happened?" Emily asked, taking him by the wrist and examining his fingers.

"The damned thing bit me."

"Jonathan! You're bleeding!"

It was true. More confused than anything else, Jonathan stared at the thin line of red across the base of his thumb. He pulled his hand away and sucked on the bite. "Imagine that," he said wonderingly. "Vicious ducks. You don't suppose that was what that waiter was trying to tell us about. . . ."

"Let's get back to the room," Emily said. She threw the last of the bread into the mass of quacking bills and twitching rumps, then turned away. "Jonathan?"

He shook himself from his reverie and followed her. "Yes, dear. Coming." But as he took one last glance across his shoulder, the huge mallard seemed to be watching him, gazing deep into his eyes with a look that was both angry and somehow sorrowful at the same time.

A month later, back in Connecticut, Jonathan had returned to his accounting firm, and Emily was settling into the routines of housework. As was common in those days, they'd married without having slept together beforehand, let alone having lived together, and they were still getting to know each other. Thus the things that Emily began to discover among her husband's belongings did not alarm her.

Not at first.

Things like the down pillows he'd bought to replace the foam rubber ones she preferred. The half-eaten crusts of stale bread that she'd found on the floor around his desk in the study, where he'd been working late at night with increasing regularity. Frankie Laine's "Cry of the Wild Goose" left on the changer of the hi-fi. The decoys in the garage. A shirt with a print featuring hunters and hunting horns, torn to shreds and left on the bottom of the closet.

His behavior seemed to be changing as well. He grew more restless every day, more prone to sudden fits of clumsiness. Though it had always been one of his favorite meals during their courtship, he now refused to eat chicken or any other poultry. Even the sight of fried eggs seemed to horrify him.

They had been married just two days less than a month when it began in earnest.

They were lying in bed together, a gentle autumn breeze tugging at the window curtains. Emily was just about to fall asleep when she heard Jonathan shifting around in the bed.

"Is something wrong?" she asked him sleepily.

"No, nothing. I'm just restless. I think maybe I'll get up for a while—maybe read or something."

"Jonathan?"

"What?"

"Are you . . . all right? You've seemed so distant lately. Is there anything bothering you? Is there something wrong with me?" Emily had been paying attention to the commercials on television lately, and it had begun to make her insecure.

"No, darling, of course not." He took her into his arms and patted her back, but she could tell that his heart was not entirely in it. "You go back to sleep," he said. "I'll just go read for a while."

She did fall asleep, at least for a few minutes, but then a sudden noise woke her again. It came from the direction of the study, and it sounded like a strangled cough, or a . . .

No. Emily suppressed the thought before it could fully form. There was no way a bird that large could actually get inside the house.

She got up and slipped into her dressing gown. She hated to disturb him, but she knew she wouldn't be able to go back to sleep until she was sure Jonathan was all right. She tiptoed down the hall, hesitated with her hand on the knob of the study door, then eased it open.

Enough moonlight shone through the open window for Emily to see that her husband wasn't there. She was about to move on and check the kitchen when something caught her attention.

She turned on the overhead light and gasped. Jonathan's robe and pyjamas lay in a tangled heap in the middle of the floor.

There was no other sign of her husband in the room. Her heart in her throat, she searched the rest of the house, fruitlessly, and came back to the study.

That was when she noticed the feathers on the sill of the open window.

Frightened, but knowing she had to make the effort, she walked around the outside of the house with a flashlight.

The neighbors all lived on the far side of the woods, and Emily felt threatened by the lurking trees and the ghostly moonlight reflecting off the pond. She couldn't find as much as a footprint to show that Jonathan had been outside, so she went back in, locking the front door after her.

Latching windows and bolting doors as she went, she made another search of the house, calling Jonathan's name. Then she returned to the living room and sat on the couch, holding the flashlight in one hand and the fireplace poker in the other.

She thought for a long time about phoning the police, but she knew there was nothing they could do before morning. Maybe Jonathan would be back by then, with an explanation for everything.

Please, God, she prayed, let him be back by then. . . .

The living room clock read five A.M. when she heard something at the other end of the house. It sounded like someone trying to get in the window of the bedroom.

Oh God, Emily thought. The latch on that window is loose. Jonathan had been meaning to fix it.

She started down the hall, holding the poker in front of her. Better to face it, she thought, whatever it is, than to let it find me cowering under the sofa.

At the door of the bedroom she stopped.

Jonathan lay in the bed, asleep.

The window with the weakened latch was open, and the prints of bare, dirty feet led from there to the bed.

Emily bent over him, hearing the sound of his ragged breathing, and tried to wake him. He moaned once, but he seemed too exhausted to come around completely. Emily stretched out beside him, willing to let him sleep, grateful beyond words that she had him back.

She rocked him in her arms for several minutes, then

slowed, sniffing the air. She looked at Jonathan and sniffed again.

His breath reeked of fish.

Jonathan woke up unable to remember anything that had happened after he went to the study. He thought he might have had a dream that he was naked, trying to open a locked window.

"You were gone almost five hours," Emily told him. She was exhausted, not having slept at all.

"I must have been sleepwalking," Jonathan said.

"But where did you go? What did you do? You were alone out there, naked, for five hours!"

"I tell you I don't know," Jonathan said, with just a trace of irritation in his voice. "I just want to sleep some more. I'm so . . . tired. . . ."

Emily left him and sat on the couch in the living room, drinking one cup of coffee after another. Not even the caffeine could keep her awake, however, and by late afternoon she dozed off. She woke in Jonathan's arms as he carried her back to bed.

"Whaa . . . ?" she asked.

"Go to sleep," he told her. "Everything is fine."

It was night. The bed seemed to swallow her, and for a second Emily let herself go, back into the waiting depths of sleep. Then some part of her fought back to the surface.

"No," she murmured. "Got to stay awake."

She forced her eyes open and blinked until the room came into focus. "Jonathan?"

He was gone, and she could hear the whisper of his study door closing behind him.

She was too weak to stand, so she crawled on her hands and knees to the door of the study. Forcing herself onto her wobbling legs, she twisted the handle and flung the door wide.

And she saw him.

At first she wanted to laugh. He had taken off his clothes and was bending down in a tight crouch. His hands were tucked up into his armpits and his elbows were straining toward his sides.

And then he began to change.

"Jonathan!" she cried, but he was beyond hearing. His legs were drawing up and his feet were turning orange. Brown feathers were sprouting from his arms, and his nose was growing, flattening. . . .

"Jonathan!" she screamed. "I can't stand this! My mind is going to—"

"Quack," said Jonathan.

I felt dizzy, feverish, disoriented. Dr. Canard was obviously mad, raving, certifiable. I had listened to his story with impatience, disbelief, and finally scorn.

And yet . . .

Why had my mother refused to let me watch Daffy Duck cartoons as a child? Why had I been in junior high before I'd found out what the word "poultry" meant? Why had the sight of a friend's swim fins sent her into hysterics?

"I can't—" I began.

"You find this all hard to believe, *nicht wahr?* You think it absurd. Well, why shouldn't you? To me it seemed absurd also, when I first heard of it."

Dr. Canard stood up and began to pace the floor. He was so short that it seemed to take minutes for his tiny footsteps to carry him from one side of the room to the other. "Your parents first came to me when ordinary doctors proved stupid, useless, worthless to them." He paused to stare at me

for a second. "As they so often are. Would you believe they once thought that I—" He shook his head. "But I digress.

"The medical doctors told your father to see a psychiatrist; the psychiatrists told him that both of them should be locked up. Finally they heard of my researches, such as the salt-free diet I developed while in telepathic contact with the planet Uranus. They knew I would be the one to find the answer."

"And—"

"Did I find the answer? Of course, I did. I observed your father for months, traveled over the Continent, researching folk tales and poring over ancient volumes in obscure libraries. Your father was a remarkable case. You have heard of the legend of the werewolf? Yes, I see that you have. Well, your father was—"

"No . . ."

"—yes, a wereduck. That is correct."

In their third month at the clinic, Emily came to Jonathan as he was studying a moth- and mold-ravaged text entitled *The Necronomiduck.*

"I'm pregnant," she told him.

Jonathan's face lit up. "Darling, are you sure?"

She nodded, and Jonathan started to throw his arms around her, then suddenly pulled back.

"What's wrong?" she asked.

He shook his head. "Nothing. I'm sure it's nothing. It's just . . . what if the child should turn out to be a . . . a monster? Like his father?"

Emily pressed his face to her breast. "No, Jonathan! Don't say that! Don't ever say that!"

"But even if he's perfectly normal, what kind of father would he have? What kind of help would I be to you? Could he live on the fish and bread crumbs I'd bring home?"

"Oh, darling, that's not important. As long as we love each other, nothing else matters."

The boy, Drake, was born normally, and the three of them returned to Connecticut. Dr. Canard promised that he would not rest until he'd found a solution to Jonathan's affliction, but he did not sound hopeful.

It was fall again in Connecticut, and during the first full moon in October, Jonathan disappeared. Emily was frantic, phoning police and animal shelters for miles around, with no success. Finally, two days later, Jonathan returned. He was dressed in nothing but an oversized raincoat and was sneezing all the way up the path.

"I came around in a swamp in Maryland," he told her. "I had a couple of shotgun pellets in one arm from an off-season hunter. The last thing I remember before that was smelling the air and feeling this overpowering urge to fly south."

He'd stolen the raincoat from a sleeping hobo and hitch-hiked home, without even a dime to call for help.

"I can't go on this way," he told her. "Next month it'll happen again, and who knows how far I'll get before I come back to my senses?"

"I could sew up a little bag for you," Emily offered. "You could wear it around your neck, and I could put some traveler's checks in it."

Jonathan shook his head. "It's no good. I'd never remember to put it on. No, Emily. I want you to stay here with Drake, and I'll face this on my own."

"If you have to go," Emily said, "you have to go. I'll manage. But what about you? You can't just wander the world, leading some kind of desperate hand-to-bill existence?"

"Somewhere there's an answer," Jonathan said. "I'll find it, and when I do, I'll come back to you."

Emily never gave up hope. Each spring she sat on the porch with field glasses, watching the ragged V's of ducks as they crossed the sky, waiting for her husband. Each fall, with the first frost, she aged an entire year in a day.

Sixteen years passed, and her son grew almost to manhood. And then, one day, a letter arrived from Mexico, covered with exotic stamps and addressed in a familiar hand.

"I have it here somewhere," said Dr. Canard, shuffling through the drawers of his desk. "Ach, here it is."

I had been hoping he wouldn't be able to find it. The more elaborate his story got, the more nervous it made me, and when he started producing evidence, the urge to run away came over me again.

"I'll read you some parts of it," Canard said. " 'My darling, I long to . . .' No, not that part. Ach, here we are.

This last winter was so cold that I came all the way to Mexico, to a small village in the Sonoran Desert. I met an old man here, a crazy hermit. All the people in town think he's a witch, but he seemed to understand me somehow, to know about my "problem" without my telling him. He speaks very good English—he says he learned it from an American anthropologist who comes to visit him every couple of years and make up stories about him.

We'd stay up late into the night, him eating cactus and me munching on bits of stale tortillas, and he made me see something I'd never thought of. I'd been trying to run away from my curse instead of learning to live with it. He taught me to embrace it, to accept it totally, and then, when he told me what he could do for me—for us—I realized that this was the answer I'd been searching for.

"So," Dr. Canard said, popping the monocle out of his eye, "your mother joined him in Mexico. She could not tell you what it was she planned to do, first because she could not know if it would be successful, and second because she knew you would not believe her anyway."

"Did—"

"Did this witch doctor cure your father, you ask? Yes, he did. Your father no longer changes to a duck with the full moon."

He paused dramatically, and I knew the worst was about to come. "Now," he proclaimed, "he—and your mother—are *ducks forever!*"

Canard ran to the glass doors and yanked open the curtains, exposing the two huge ducks who had been waiting there the entire time.

"Behold, Drake Russel!" Canard shouted. "Your mother and father!"

I let the silence hang on for a long time, and then I said, very quietly, "You're completely wacko, you know. Bananas. Berkshire. Round the bend. Stark, staring—"

"So it must seem to you, my boy—"

"Shut up!" My hands were shaking as I got out of the chair, and for a second I thought I was going to shove the monocle down the old man's throat. "I don't want to hear any more, do you understand me?"

"You know it is the truth. That is why you are so frightened of it."

"I'm not frightened!" I shouted, grabbing one of the end

tables and swinging it back like a club. "I'm fine! Stay away from me!" I started backing toward the door.

Canard held out his hands. "Drake, listen, I must warn you—"

"No!" I yelled, throwing the table and running out the door. I ran all the way to the village and took the next flight home to Connecticut.

I write this at my father's desk. Next to me is a book entitled *Lycanthropy: A Symposium,* and next to it are perhaps a dozen others on the same subject.

I do not believe Dr. Canard's preposterous story. I do not believe in werewolves, wereducks, were-elephants or were-fish.

And yet . . .

I have read all of my father's books on the subject— brought them down from where they were hidden in the attic and studied them. The books tell me that the curse of the werewolf is passed on to the eldest son on his eighteenth birthday.

Tomorrow, on the night of the full moon, I will turn eighteen. Is it only the power of suggestion that has been leading me out for long walks beside my father's fish pond, or is it only the beginning of something far, far worse?

Voices in the Wind

Elizabeth S. Helfman

AT THE WINDOW of his cottage by the sea sat old Tom Anthony. His eyes were in a dream, and he held his head a little to one side, listening, it seemed, to something far away but very pleasant to his hearing. His wife, Sarah, set down a bowl of sauerkraut on the table in the center of the room. She felt suddenly very lonely. There sat Tom, as he had every afternoon and evening, ever since he had been too old to go out fishing. It was worse for her than when he used to be away all day. Then she had expected no companionship. Only occasionally he would come home with a lost look in his eyes and a fantastic tale of the wind and the sea on his lips. She would forgive him, and laugh. And he laughed with her.

He was so different now, content to merely sit and listen to nothing. It was strange, too, that he no longer sought out old Jonah, who lived across the fence at the south. So often, before, they would tell and retell long tales of the sea and hazardous fishing.

"Tom, your supper is ready."

She had called him just like this for so many days. He

came, as she had known he would, slowly, with a look of childlike apology. "I ought to be more talkative, I suppose, Sarah. I'm sorry."

They sat at the table in silence, and the food stood waiting. Time hesitated for a moment, then went on again. Sarah was a little afraid.

"Tom, why do you sit at the window every day, so long, staring out and looking lost, as if you were listening to something? You seem so far away, you might as well be miles out at sea."

Tom looked at her apologetically. "I'm sorry, Sarah, and I'd tell you but you'd think me crazy."

"I'll think you worse than crazy if you go on this way, Tom. Tell me!"

Tom leaned his elbows on the table so suddenly that the candle flame trembled. The shadows in the corner of the room drew back. "All right, Sarah, I'll tell you."

Sarah bent forward eagerly. "Yes, Tom."

"It's the wind, Sarah, and the sea."

"Tom, haven't you heard enough of the wind and the sea all your life without spending hour after hour listening to them now?"

"It's different now, Sarah. I never knew until some weeks ago that the wind has words to say when it runs about outside the house and cries and moans around the corners. If you listen long enough you can hear what the sea, too, is saying as it comes tumbling in, one wave after another."

Sarah's face was blank. But Tom kept on.

"It tells secrets to the old pines, Sarah."

"You *are* crazy, Tom Anthony."

"Why shouldn't the wind say something, Sarah, when it goes crying about, always restless, as if it were searching for something?"

172 •

He *is* crazy, thought Sarah. The thought went through her head over and over again, dully, like a headache.

"I said you'd call me crazy, Sarah."

What should she do with him now? she wondered.

"Come with me to the window and listen," he begged.

"Tom, it's witches, or—or something. Oh, Tom! *Are* you crazy?"

He was silent; then he sighed a little and finished eating. The same thought went through Sarah's head over and over again—what should she do?

Of course Sarah did nothing about it. Somehow thinking that Tom was a little crazy did not make things much different from what they were before. Only now he pleaded with her every evening to come with him to the window and listen. He wanted so much for her to believe.

At last one evening she went to the window with him and sat there a long time, her hand in his, listening.

"Do you hear them, Sarah?"

"Yes, I hear them, not being deaf. But no words, Tom, no words."

He was disappointed, but he was not less confident. "Listen again," he said.

She listened. "No words, Tom."

Nevertheless, after that she went to the window with him every evening, to sit there quietly and listen, even if there were no words to hear. She felt closer to Tom that way, and she was sure he felt closer to her. On evenings when there was no wind she could feel the loneliness in them both.

Sarah had almost forgotten that she thought Tom crazy. And yet, when she took time to think about it, she supposed he must be a little simple-minded. For she could not hear words in the wind's moaning, nor a message in the sea's murmurs.

"Can't you hear them, Sarah? Can't you?" Tom would ask.

On an evening in July there was a wild wind wandering about the house, and the sea roared loud on the shore. Tom left his supper before he was half finished to go to the window and listen. Sarah washed the dishes, dried them, and followed. They sat there a long time, Tom with an expression of ecstasy on his face, Sarah passive and rather tired. The wind and the sea roared, echoed each other, roared again. Suddenly an expression of wonder and a kind of terror came to Sarah's face.

"Tom!"

She seized his arm.

"Tom, I thought I heard—"

Tom was not disturbed, not surprised. A triumphant smile spread over his face.

"Of course you heard them, Sarah."

She was silent again, listening. What was it the wind said? She couldn't be sure. Oh, it was all nonsense. And yet . . .

"Tom, am I crazy, too?"

He laughed. "It doesn't matter—if we *both* are—does it?"

She could hear only a word now and then, but there was no denying it. After a while she grew weary of sitting there and went to bed, a little afraid but very happy. Tom followed much later, softly whistling a strange tune she had never heard before.

Sarah had to listen many times, hour after hour, while the wind went around the house, before she was sure of the words it used. She was almost as eager to listen as Tom, though she always washed the dishes and put them away before she went to the window.

One night, when they were listening together, the words

of the wind came clearer than ever before. They made a chant like this;

"The wind is wild with wandering,
Wild with moaning through the trees,
Wild with whispering in the pines,
Wild with crying to the sea. . . .

"The wind is wild with wandering,
Over the troubled sea again,
Whistling around the house again.
I am the wind,
The wandering wind."

Sarah smiled somewhat foolishly and murmured, " 'The wind is wild with wandering.' Who could have known . . . ?"

Tom was listening to still other words, for a gentle rain was falling. And he heard the rain say:

"I come with murmurs,
Murmurs,
Out of the clouds that know the thunder,
Out of the sea that roars and tumbles,
Down to the earth that waits and wonders—
I am the murmuring rain."

"The rain sings, too, Sarah," Tom said.

The rain kept on murmuring. The wind in its wandering blew open the door, put out the candle, and left Tom and Sarah in sudden darkness. He took her hand in his and they stood there in that darkness, silent and unafraid.

There was a day in late July when an unexpected rain came out of a sky that had been still and blue an hour before. Tom and Sarah were at the window, listening to what the angry rain might say, when there was a knock at the door. Sarah was afraid—why she did not know.

"I won't go, Tom. I won't."

He crossed to the door and opened it. On the doorstep stood a teenage boy, wet all over, with little rivulets running from the ends of his long, blond hair.

Tom recognized him—Oliver Trowbridge, from the nearby summer resort. He had taken Oliver sailing many times and let him dangle a line over the edge of the boat until he caught a fish or two.

Oliver ambled in, past Tom, to the fireplace, where Tom had built a roaring fire against the dampness. "Whew!" he said. "I thought you'd never get to the door. I got soaked in all this rain, and I thought you'd let me dry off for a minute or two."

Suddenly Sarah hated Oliver Trowbridge. He had come just when she had been listening to catch a few words the rain said. Now he stood there by the fire as if it were his own, babbling things she had no patience with. But she said only, "You're welcome here. Would you like something to eat?" And she brought out a dish of her sauerkraut.

"Oh," said Oliver. "Thanks." After a slow start he ate it eagerly.

Sarah saw that Tom was at the window looking out, no longer listening to Oliver. And yet she knew he was not content to have him there.

"What's the matter with the old man?" Oliver gulped his last mouthful. "Is he deaf?"

"No, he's not deaf. He's listening to things you'd be glad to hear, if you could."

"Oh, of course. Yes, of course," Oliver drawled. Then he

smiled and crossed to the window, where he stood beside Tom. He put one hand on Tom's shoulder and received no answer. He touched Tom's shoulder, again with no success. Feeling playful, he pulled Tom's ear, very gently.

Tom turned to him angrily. "What do you want with me?"

Oliver answered, "I want to know what it is you're listening to."

"You won't believe, but if you want to know—I listen to what the wind says, what the sea mumbles, what the rain murmurs when it comes out of the clouds."

Oliver laughed long and loud. "Well, let me listen with you, old man."

Tom turned back to the window. Oliver stood beside him, minute after minute. Then he said, "All I hear is a little bit of rain falling, a little bit of ocean coming in, the way it always does, and the wind blowing around. No words."

"I wouldn't expect *you* to hear them."

"Does your wife hear them?"

Sarah nodded emphatically. "Of course."

Oliver broke again into shrill laughter, then stopped as suddenly as he had begun. "Well, I'll be going. The rain's about over. But first, let me tell you this—if you really think you hear any words in the sound of wind, and rain, and sea, you are absolutely crazy. Absolutely."

Tom turned to the window again, as if he wished he had not heard. Sarah smiled to herself, as if she knew things Oliver could never dream of. And he mistook her smile.

"Oh, I suppose you've been fooling all this time," he said. "You *were* clever. For a while I thought you really meant it. Time to go. Good-bye, everybody!" And he was gone.

"What a fool!" said Sarah. Tom nodded in agreement. "Of course *he* couldn't hear the voices, not even wanting to believe."

"Of course not."

They went to listen again and heard the wind murmuring,

"I am the wind,
The wind that murmurs in the pines."

They were troubled, though. Tom felt for the first time that it would be pleasant to hear someone besides Sarah and himself swear to the truth of the words in the wind's voice. And so he sought out old Jonah the next day. He found him sitting in a corner of his kitchen, looking out to the sea and dreaming.

Jonah woke from dreaming to astonishment when he saw Tom. "Well, Tom! Where have you been all this time? I thought likely you'd fallen into the sea and drowned, or something even better!" He laughed heartily, as if this were the greatest joke in the world.

Tom shook his head. "No, I've simply been at home, listening to things."

"Well, Tom," said Jonah cheerfully, "I guess that's about all there is to do now that we can't go fishing anymore."

Tom was thoughtful. "I suppose no one around here knows more about the sea than you do, Jonah."

Jonah laughed again, finding this an even greater joke. "You're right, Tom, I reckon no one could know more about the sea than old Jonah."

"Well, have you ever heard the wind at sea telling you things?"

"Of course, and you have, too, Tom. It used to tell me when I'd better make for home instead of being caught in a storm and when it would be safe to steer north."

"But, Jonah, did the wind ever *speak* to you? Did you ever hear words in its voice?"

"Of course not, and neither did you, Tom."

"Not until a few weeks ago. But now both Sarah and I listen at the window when the wind is blowing, and it chants strange words."

Old Jonah laughed comfortably. "What a queer thing to dream about."

"It's not a dream, Jonah. We've listened hour after hour and we hear what the wind says, the sea, and the rain."

"Sarah hears this, too?"

"Both of us."

"No one knows more about the sea and the wind than I do, and I never heard any words. You're getting old, Tom, getting old. And so is Sarah. Perhaps you've both become a little simple. That makes me sad. You used to be one of the best fishermen on the coast."

That night there was again a wind, and Tom and Sarah went to listen to its song. But they remembered Oliver with his scornful laughter, and the careless disbelief of old Jonah. Tom heard some of the words the wind said, but Sarah's thoughts were so busy that she heard none of them.

The night after that there was also a wind. Tom and Sarah were troubled as they sat at supper.

"He was a fool, that Oliver person," grumbled Tom. "And old Jonah, he's a good enough old man, but he can't have listened to the wind for very long."

Sarah nodded. "Oliver was crazy. And old Jonah pretty near it, I guess."

"And yet," said Tom, suddenly thoughtful, "are they crazy or are we? Have we been wrong all the time?"

Sarah, too, grew thoughtful. "I don't know, Tom."

"Why, we've been right, haven't we, Sarah?"

"I suppose so, Tom."

Sarah remembered that she was, above all, a sensible woman. And yet—surely she had heard what the wind said.

"Aren't you *sure,* Sarah?"

"Yes, Tom, of course."

There was silence for a moment.

"Sarah, you don't sound so sure."

"Well, Tom, perhaps I'm not, after all."

"Do you think we *are* a little crazy?"

"Oh, Tom, I don't know." And she didn't. Perhaps they were right, perhaps wrong; likelier wrong, and yet she'd rather be right. Why did Tom keep asking such questions?

"Look, Sarah, the way to be sure is to go to the window now and listen. Come with me."

She went willingly with him, and they stood a long time listening. At first she thought she heard a word or two in the wind's voice. Then she thought, and in a minute was sure, that she was hearing nothing but inarticulate sounds.

"I don't hear the wind saying anything, Tom."

The look on his face told her that he, too, had heard nothing.

"Oh, just a minute, Sarah. Perhaps . . ."

Again they listened, while the inarticulate wind wandered about outside.

"Perhaps what, Tom?"

There was a silence in which even the wind made no sound.

"I don't know, Sarah."

"Tom," Sarah said. "It was a beautiful dream we had together."

The cry of the wind had ceased, and the sound of the sea as it murmured seemed very far away.

About the Editors

America's most prolific author, **Isaac Asimov** has written over four hundred books on a variety of subjects—from math and physics to the Bible and Shakespeare. Winner of five Hugo Awards and three Nebulas (including one naming him a Grand Master of Science Fiction), Dr. Asimov is perhaps best known for the international bestsellers *Foundation's Edge* and *The Robots of Dawn*. He has also written more than seventy children's books, including the popular Norby books coauthored with wife, Janet. Asimov writes from 8 A.M. to 5 P.M., seven days a week, in a secluded two-room office lined with more than two thousand books. He lives in New York City.

Martin H. Greenberg has compiled over three hundred anthologies in the mystery, science fiction, fantasy, horror, and western genres. Over eighty of his anthologies were co-compiled with Isaac Asimov. He has been published in eleven languages by major publishers, and currently lives in Green Bay, Wisconsin.

About the Artist

The exciting fantasy illustrations of **Larry Elmore** are indeed a product of his childhood. He was enchanted as a young boy growing up near the lush forests, steep hills, and deep valleys surrounding his rural Kentucky home. And he continually sought out his older relatives to hear their tall tales and ghost stories that fueled his imagination enough to start drawing whenever he found time.

Now a successful free-lance artist who holds a bachelor's degree in fine arts from Western Kentucky University, Larry's fantasy illustrations have appeared in many books. After living in Lake Geneva, Wisconsin, for eight years, the artist has recently returned to his Kentucky home.

"I know that the land will enhance and deepen the emotions I experienced as a child," he says, "emotions that existed in a world of mystery and where fantasies came true. Those are feelings I try to capture in my art."